Wet Storage and Other Stories

by

C. C. Alick

Thank you
Charlie Williams
Claude

authorHOUSE™

1663 LIBERTY DRIVE, SUITE 200
BLOOMINGTON, INDIANA 47403
(800) 839-8640
WWW.AUTHORHOUSE.COM

This book is a work of fiction. People, places, events, and situations are the product of the author's imagination. Any resemblance to actual persons, living or dead, or historical events, is purely coincidental.

© 2005 C. C. Alick. All Rights Reserved.

No part of this book may be reproduced, stored in a retrieval system, or transmitted by any means without the written permission of the author.

First published by AuthorHouse 07/20/05

ISBN: 1-4208-5208-6 (sc)

Printed in the United States of America
Bloomington, Indiana

This book is printed on acid-free paper.

CONTENTS

Window On The World 1
Mumbo Jumbo 22
Walking In Memphis 29
Redemption Songs 48
Toetags 79
Far From Shore 98
Beat Me 107
The Visitor 118
Wet Storage 127

WINDOW ON THE WORLD

No one told me I could be seduced by money. If they had, I would not have understood or believed it. Being the first person in my family to acquire an advanced degree, I'm burdened by the notion that I should have use it for more than acquiring wealth.

These last ten years slipped around me like a benevolent snake and I'm still in its coils. Women came and went, cities blended into an amalgamation of lodgings. I was fresh out of the University of the West Indies in Jamaica when I landed my first job with Mayfield Hotels International. Young fellow from Grenada suddenly placed in the proximity of affluence. The sheer material comfort was immediately intoxicating.

The woman in the human resource department told me she loved my accent. Where was it from? I told her Grenada and her face lit up. She had been on a cruise to the Isle of Spice. She favored me because she had pleasant memories of the place where I was born. What a thing! My first assignment, as a concierge paid three times what my father made at his job. It took me three years to become an assistant manager. When they offered me a position as a Trouble Shooter, I jumped at the occasion, not knowing what a pain in the ass the whole thing would be. It was like constantly inheriting virulent conditions. First, you had to hunt down the thieves, drug dealers, and con artists, get rid of them without getting the hotel's name in the newspaper, then you put a new team in place. Two days before, I had completed an assignment in Memphis and was awaiting orders from headquarters. The telephone call from my father's wife caught me by surprise.

"Cammy, you have to come home," she said, without greetings or salutations.

"What's wrong, Enid?"

"It's your father, Cammy. I don't want to tell you everything on this phone. We're all longing to see you. You have been away far too long. Your friend Goday is making quite the name for himself."

Mentioning Goday was the height of trickery on her part. She knew that I hadn't written him a single letter in the ten years I've been abroad. She deliberately baited me with silence.

"What's wrong with daddy, Enid?"

"He lost his voice, cammy. That's all I'm going to tell you. Come home, he's sick, bad. Okay?" and she hangup without allowing me to make any objection.

I was left grasping with the residue she left behind. I couldn't imagine Hezekiah without a voice. The Greatest Liar in the World unable to speak? I felt like a man who had been knocked out and was now regaining consciousness. Memories of the place she had called from now seemed as patchy as the old clothes worn by the street people I frequently instructed the doorman to chase away from the portico of our hotels. What kind of story would my father construe from the particulars of my life in the last ten years?

Hezekiah was like the shadows that creep across the ground, the ones cast by clouds drifting across the sun. So many of our exchanges from my youth remained beneath my skin. They itched, a convergence of blood connecting me to this summons from this man they nicknamed the Greatest Liar in the World, and a village perched on a hill.

The place was like an untamed garden, grasses, shrubs; they lined a narrow dirt path up the side of a hill to a cluster of board houses. The lodgings sheltered geraniums, frangipanis and hibiscus; all watered by rains decanting off galvanized roofs. In reminiscence, these plants are forever in bloom.

This place on the hill overlooked acres and acres of sugar cane. To the north and south, the cane fields stretched out to stands of briar, mahogany, and banyan trees. My father took me hunting in that bush twice. He said the shrieks were just birds, doves, cobos, and piperits, supported by iguanas and other lizards crawling over dry leaves. But I knew better. Because in those trees, I saw places where the light never reached the ground and the shadows danced like skin on bones.

A man named Winston Bonaparte came to Morne Jaloux and married a beautiful young woman with one short leg. To this day, I'm still trying to comprehend why his appearance affected my life so deeply. He was a big man. He came from a village called Belmont, down near the ocean. He was the one who first nicknamed my father.

My father silently resented Winston Bonaparte for linking the word "lie" to his name. But Winston meant no insult. Even I knew that. My father frequently sat in the shade of the coconut and the breadfruit trees; he would let loose his raw notions on anyone who paused too long.

My stepmother, Enid, we almost became friends once. That was the day she told me how she fell in love with my father. "He told me one of his yarns, and it made my heart beat faster", she said. "That was the beginning." And she laughed bashfully. It came more from her eyes because her hand was about to cover her mouth.

My father told me stories that made my skin crawl, things that prowl the night, things that I have only in recent years gained the courage to call by name. He spoke of these creatures with ease and grace, placing himself at the center of the action. He had seen and had full knowledge of all their deeds.

In my imagination, all the scamps that my father spoke about came out of the woods across the cane and made their way to Morne Jaloux. In the dark of night, the dogs were the first to sense them. They warned us with their yelps, howls and frequently they snarled at naked air.

At the near edge of the great field of cane sat the old bellowing sugar works, churning, belching and vomiting the vats of juice that will soon be molasses, sugar and rum. The miasma from the raw cane saturated the air around the factory. I remember the vapors entering my nose and leaving a sweet taste at the back of my tongue. Even now, the memory is sweet.

The men of Morne Jaloux made their living in that factory and from those fields of cane. In the entire village, my father was the only man to put on a suit and tie for work. That allowed him some respect, although he was just a clerk in the shipping department of George F. Huggins and Company.

Winston Bonaparte was twenty the year the Government hired him and some other men to widen the path that led from the pavement near Miss Darling's dry goods shop to the houses on the hill. He entered the good graces of the people of Morne Jaloux one rain-soaked day.

One of the trucks hauling materials slid off the road and pinned a man up to his neck in the mud under its wheels. Try as they might, they could not free him. They kept digging the sludge away from his face, but it would flow right back, almost covering his nose. The truck was stuck deep in the black soil, unwieldy against the trunks of two large mahoganies. Only one person could squeeze in to gain a firm grip on the vehicle's frame. Someone advanced the idea to push the truck out, but that would have crushed or probably suffocate the buried man.

By now a large crowd had gathered. In the crowd was Idona Redhead, the young woman with one short leg. Winston had been trying to get her attention. He saw this as his one true occasion. He waded into the mud and wedged himself under the frame. Those closest to him swear that they heard a fart. Everyone else heard a terrible grunt. The vehicle moved just enough for the others to pull the man out. The crowd declared Winston Bonaparte's new name would be Sampson. "No!" shouted young Winston. "I'm the Jawbone." And the name stuck. From that day on, everybody called him Jawbone.

Tragedy followed Idona Redhead like a trained dog. She was born to Melda and Justin Redhead. Polio shriveled her leg when she was a little girl. Idona was fifteen years old when rain dislodged a huge chunk of rock from its resting place on the side of a hill. The rock careened down the incline and smashed into the bus in which she was traveling with her parents. The pieces were scattered into a steep ravine, killing everyone, except Idona. People started whispering about Obeah and the Redhead family.

After the hospital stay, Idona came back to Morne Jaloux, and everyone embraced her. She planted potatoes, yams, and she harvested the breadfruits growing on the ground around the house she inherited from her parents. She sold these provisions in the market at Saint Georges and did well. Idona lived a solitary life, protected by the rumors of Obeah and the fears of the men, and boys of Morne Jaloux.

Winston Bonaparte, the man who called himself Jawbone, started wooing her and no one warned him about her curse. They saw Jawbone as the one chance for some happiness in her life. The wedding was a great event in Morne Jaloux. Idona was the only bride with sixteen mothers. A year later, a child was born;

they called him Manuel. He had his mother's graceful features and the best parts of his father's physique.

Everyone soon realized Jawbone had two personas, one sober and another prone to violence when drunk. Sometimes Idona would appear with bruises on her face, but no one interfered because most of the men of Morne Jaloux, at one time or another, found it necessary to bully their wives.

My father scorned such behavior. I'll never forget the day that Stumpy's mother, Miss Lashley, came to see my stepmother, Enid. Her face looked bumpy, and inflated, her eyes red from tears. Enid brought a tray with two cups of black sage tea. Miss Lashley wanted advice: should she have her brothers and father run her husband out of Morne Jaloux for beating her too often?

My father looked at Enid before he took my two brothers and me outside. "That's no way to handle a woman." He had this way of wrinkling his forehead and arching his mouth before saying serious stuff. "A real man should never have to beat his woman. You see your mother and me? I give her what she desires and she gives me what I want. Simple exchange. We respect each other." I had an inkling that things were not as simple between women and men as my father would have me believe. But I never doubted him.

My father reserved his most stringent contempt for the behavior of Jawbone and that of his friends from Belmont. Lazy hooligans, he called them, drinking rum, carousing at the house up the road, eating all of Idona's food. Every weekend.

Sometimes the police came, but then never arrested anyone. My father told me drinking rum was for fools.

"Why do you think they called it a spirit? You put that stuff in your belly; it stifles your soul, replacing it with rot."

The most famous fight to occur at Jawbone's house was between him and a man name Quash. Their argument started over whom was the better Calypso Singer? The Mighty Sparrow or Lord Melody? How they came to blows was never conveyed to me, but Jawbone hit Quash with his bare fist on the top of the head. He hit him so hard that everyone thought Jawbone had broken both the man's ankles, but nothing like that happened. However, when Quash recovered from the concussion, he developed a stutter that remains with him to this day.

Manuel Bonaparte, Jawbone and Idona's son was the only kid in Morne Jaloux with no siblings. He lived in the small house with his mother and his father. I lived just down the road with my mother, my father and my two younger brothers. How Manuel and me became the best of friends is a story that you will learn in the bye and bye.

Three structures rested on our piece of land: our house, kitchen and latrine. The latrine walls were covered with pictures from the pages of many magazines. No black faces were present on those pages. I assumed very few black people populated the world outside Grenada.

The tourist boats that docked at Saint Georges confirmed my suspicions. Black people never came. Sometimes Manuel, Stumpy, Selwyn and I would wait at the pavement near Miss Darling's shop. The taxis carrying the visitors would slow down to make the corner. We would wave and shout at the white people inside the cars. My father would have killed me if he'd seen me. Frequently they threw coins at us. I'll never forget the time a handful came flying out of a car and struck me in the face, leaving a dent on my forehead before they jingled down the pavement. I didn't get hold of one, Stumpy and Manuel got most of them. The other guys grabbed the rest before I could regain my composure. I was left fingering that mark on my head.

Everyone called Manuel, Goday. He inherited the nickname from the Prime Minister to Charles the Fourth of Spain, who ruled that country during the lifetime of the famous Spanish painter Francisco Goya.

Manuel's Father, Jawbone, had seen a movie about a conflict called the War of The Orange, fought between Spain and Portugal many centuries before. The picture depicted a scene where The Prime Minister, a fellow called "Godoy", presented an orange branch from some village he had liberated to the Queen of Spain, Maria Luisa, who gave him the title The Prince of Peace. Jawbone was so moved by the scene that he decided to nickname his son after the Prime Minister.

"Godoy" sounded strange coming out of the mouth of a West Indian. You see, in the local vernacular the letter A is sacred. In words where they are no A's, one might be thrown in just for flavor. That's how Manuel Bonaparte became Goday instead of Godoy.

As a boy, of fifteen, I went to school and tried my best to dodge the bullies. Looking back at that time now, it all seems so simple. The men, bullied by overseers and owners in the cane fields, came home and browbeat their wives and children. Then the big boys intimidated small boys, and woe to the girls who got in the way. So, the go-around went around. The event that would remove me from that circle of violence fell from the air like a dry leaf.

We were a bunch of young gamblers, Cecil, Selwyn, Stumpy, Goday, and I; we were the players. The others would join in now and then, or sit under the coconut trees and watch. Marbles were our articles of trade and we played for keeps.

In our group, the dregs of glass were limited. If someone went broke, he had to come up with money to make a purchase from the person willing to sell to him. Saint Georges was far away and new marbles down there were several dollars per dozen.

The game went this way. A circle, called the ring, was drawn and each player placed what's called a mib into it. The object was to knock mibs out of the ring with the taw. This was accomplished through a combination of throwing the taw at the mibs in the circle from a specified distance, and then cradling the taw between the index finger and the thumb to fire at the mibs. If a player's taw became stranded in the ring, he had to put down another mib to retrieve it.

On this particular day, I was hot. I won most of the mibs and even a couple of taws that could not be retrieved. All the guys stood around gauging; they had never seen me play like that before.

Stumpy never thought he should lose and sit down like everybody else. He was big and strong and he never let us forget it. He played good soccer, but he was terrible at marbles. He had fat fingers, which made it difficult for him to deliver the taw accurately. I won his last two marbles with ease. Every time he went broke, he would try to get his marbles back without paying a penny. Usually he did it through ploys that consisted of frightening, cajoling, or wheedling the winner into being his friend. This time I was the winner and decided Stumpy would not have his way with me. I was not the biggest of the boys, but I knew how to run.

"Camy, you played like a boss today," Stumpy said, smiling, cocking his head to one side and looking at me the way a lizard looks at a fly.

"No, Stumpy, I'm not lending you anything."

"Mr. Quash will send me down to Miss Darling's for a pint of rum tonight. He buys one every Saturday. He'll give me a quarter and I'll give you a nickel. Let me have five? And my cat's-eye taw back. Then I'll give you a dime instead."

Ten cents could buy a whole heap of candy from Miss Darling. But could I trust Stumpy to fork over the money later? I didn't think so.

"No, Stumpy."

"What's wrong with you? You afraid to lose?"

"It's getting late, Stumpy, I already won. I don't want to play any more."

I turned to put some distance between us, but he reached out and grabbed the collar of my shirt from behind. As I dangled in his clutch and he spun me around, I heard a voice. Relief hit me, a kind of warmth in the blood pounding around my heart.

"Let him go, Stumpy."

Stumpy turned to face the voice, with me still in his grasp. He looked at Goday, then he chucked me aside like a bundle of cane. The expression on Stumpy's face could have melted rocks. Goday was not the biggest of us, certainly not as strapping as Stumpy, but he stood there, relaxed, as if nothing was happening.

"You think you bad, hah?" Stumpy said, moving on Goday. "Jawbone not here to help you. I'm going to thump you till you cry for your mother and piss your pants."

I spotted two ironstones near the base of the coconut tree. I edged closer to them, thinking all the time, if stumpy kicks Goday's ass and comes for me, and I can't see a clear path to run, I'm going to bust his head with both rocks.

All of us moved back. I looked around for adults, but there were none in sight. What happened next was the most beautiful thing I had ever seen. Stumpy threw a right punch at Goday. Goday ducked under it and closed in. Both his fists landed hard on Stumpy's stomach, the right, then the left, in rapid succession. Stumpy stumbled back, coughing and trying to catch his breath. Goday didn't allow him to breathe. He came again and punched Stumpy hard on the face. Blood bubbled from Stumpy's nose and down the front of his shirt. His eyes watered and he started breathing like a cow. He looked surprised. His knees buckled and he started to sway. Finally, Goday punched him on the side of his head near his ears and he went down. Cecil and I rushed Goday as he raised his foot to kick Stumpy. I was surprised by what Cecil did. He was frequently Stumpy's victim, yet he saved him from being kicked like a dog.

We left Stumpy on the ground and scattered. Goday and I went to my house where we found my father sitting under the plum tree with my younger brothers. I wanted

Wet Storage and Other Stories

to tell them what Goday had just done to Stumpy, but my father was busy attempting to acquaint my brothers with Mama Malady, that demon that carries all the diseases in the world and appears like a big, fat sheep. I knew that one well. Once or twice a week, when I was small, it would pass near our house at night.

"Those roads between the cane, after dark, not the place to walk." My father spoke those words and stared at Goday and me as if searching for something in our eyes.

"I was coming back from Springs one night. This was long before I met your mother. I had a girlfriend down there. Your grandfather had warned me about crossing the cane after dark, but I didn't listen. There was a full moon; everything looked as bright as day. Nothing to fear. Halfway home, I heard a noise. At first, it sounded like some animal dying. Aaahhhhh, aahhhh, aaahhh.

"The sound reached my ears, and the hairs on the back of my neck stood straight up. My feet, my heart, everything stopped for just an instant. Then my heart started beating hard against my chest. Babump, babump, babump. I knew I was hearing Mama Malady." He whispered the last two words, paused and looked around. "I thought of turning around and running, but then I got confused and couldn't tell if the moaning was coming from behind me or in front, but it was closing in. Aaahhh. Uhhhmm.

"I decided to hide, remain quiet. I crawled over the mound on the side of the road into the gutter near the edge of the cane. A chunk of cloud drifted over the moon. I closed my eyes tight, folded my arms around me and sat down. The grass felt damp on my ass through the seat of my pants. A disgusting odor hit me. It was as stink as a dead dog filled with maggots in the hot sun. The moaning filled my head and echoed as if someone threw me inside a big drum and started pounding on it. I could hear nothing, but Aaaah, uhhhmm, Aaaah.

"I told myself: keep those eyes closed, keep those eyes closed, don't say a word, don't make a sound. Even a sigh could mean sickness and even death. The odor ripened in my nose, I tasted it along my tongue. It coated my throat and I wanted to swallow, but I knew it would make me vomit. Soft wool brushed against me. This is it; I said to myself, I should have listened to my father. But the moaning began to fade and I could hear footsteps moving off down the gutter, and something pushing the cane aside.

I stayed there a long time after Mama Malady had passed. My legs felt like jelly, my body felt like stone. Eventually I opened one eye and peeked. When I saw nothing, I crawled out of the gutter on my hands and knees. I looked both ways down the road, nothing. The moon was shining bright again. The strength came back to my legs and I ran like hell for home, not looking back once."

Goday and I wandered off the moment Daddy went silent. I decided to walk with him, halfway to his house and ask a couple of questions. I was very impressed with what he'd done to Stumpy. The moment we were out of my father's earshot, I asked Goday, "Where did you learn to fight like that? Can you teach me?"

He looked at me, and his face became serious as if he had suddenly turned into a man and I was still

Wet Storage and Other Stories

the boy. "You don't need to fight, Camy. Stick close to me. I'll tell you what my father told me. Never throw the first blow. Make the bastard miss, and then hit him three times before he can get his footing. Never lose your head, and finish it quickly. Fighting is usually in the mind. You must see yourself hitting the other person again and again." He balled up his fist and punched at the air twice.

I acted as though I understood exactly. But to me it was mind-boggling. I had asked him to teach me, but I knew I couldn't hit another person the way Goday did. If I was lucky enough to win the fight, I knew that I would feel guilty, and to lose would be painful and humiliating. I decided the best course would be to stay out of fights, as I always have.

Goday and I were lukewarm friends before the incident with Stumpy, but defending me created a bond. Now we were two matches in the same box. We walked to school together, ate lunch together. His father took us hunting with their two dogs many times. Seeing Goday with Jawbone made me covetous. The little shoves, the shadow boxing, and the way they laughed together. My father was never that warm and friendly with me.

What happened to Stumpy changed my life and no one seemed to realize it. Everybody acted as if nothing had happened. Stumpy went back to his old ways, but he avoided Goday and me. The breather lasted about two years, and then early one carnival Monday morning life took a peculiar turn.

Carnival was coming and my father was always looking for atmosphere to wrap around his tales. Here it was, the night before carnival began, and my father was trying to explain to my brothers why they couldn't get up in the early morning to follow Goday and me into Saint Georges. He spoke from one corner of his mouth as if saving the other for something more important.

"Jou Vie and old mass is no place for children. That's the only time of the year the dead leave their graves. They're covetous and vex with the living. The dead rise up in the form of Jab Jabs. Certain fellows know just how to handle these spiteful spirits. They're the ones holding the chain attached to the jab jabs. And those big sharp machetes held in the air, at the ready. You have to be very careful how you move among those spirits. You see how they look? Clothes all torn to pieces, body caked with coal dust, face white with chalk dust, and rouge, red as blood smeared on their lips. The chains dangling from their wrists and ankles, that's all they took to the grave. Those dead slaves. Now they are back for this short time, looking for vengeance and payment for all their labor in the cane.

"I was warned. Still, the first time I came face to face with a Jab Jab, I was not prepared. I looked it in the eyes. It rattled those chains, stared me down, and shouted: 'Elou alaylambay.' the handler responded: 'jab jab,' and raised his machete in the air. 'Ah want ah penny,' said the Jab Jab, 'then I'll go back to hell.'

It headed straight at me. I'll never forget those bloody eyes. The handler pulled on the chain just before the Jab Jab reached out to grab me. Your grandmother squeezed a penny into my palm, and I flung it at the Jab Jab. It snatched the money and slunk away, looking back at me over one shoulder with vicious eyes. I was told that the moment the sun rose, they all would vanish, back to their graves for another year. But I never got to see that."

Anticipation filled my head with those strange whispers that seem to come from darkness. The yearning kept me awake for most of that night. Come carnival morning, Goday and I caught the bus into Saint Georges. Jawbone had left around Midnight for Belmont to join his friends in the steel band. Around five o'clock we found the band on Halifax Street.

The morning light reflected a curious tinge of gray, burnished steel gray. The large crowd looked so anonymous, men in women's clothes, faces covered with masks. The steel band pounded out a steady beat about a woman called Matilda, as we worked our way down the narrow street to the Esplanade. Cacophony swallowed everything.

I recognized no one except Jawbone. He was up front dancing and prancing around, wearing a costume that resembled a horse. I pointed him out to Goday and goday laughed.

The contraption fitted around his waist and ribbons concealed his legs to give the appearance that he might be riding. In his right hand, he held something that resembled a lance. On closer inspection, the lance appeared to be a giant penis. In places along the route where there were groups of women, he would charge at them and the women would scatter, some throwing papier-mâché at him. Goday and I laughed and slapped each other on the back.

For about an hour we danced to the music and laughed at the antics. Around five-thirty, a huge fracas broke out between Belmont and Sauteurs. The two bands reached Granby Street at the same time and both refused to yield. I could see fists flying and men grappling each other. Goday and I pushed forward to get a better view; we didn't want to miss a good fight. But before we could get a close look, the crowd pulled back and we saw Jawbone slumped on the pavement near the sidewalk, his costume broken and a big pool of blood at his side. Goday rushed through the crowd to his father, knelt down and shook him twice.

"Daddy, Daddy. Help me, Camy. We have to get him up, take him home. A doctor can fix him, he's just drunk."

There was a desperate look in Goday's eyes as he knelt near the unconscious body. We tried to lift Jawbone; he felt heavy and cold. Two men pulled us away as the police and an ambulance came.

A part of Idona died with Jawbone. Some of his friends from Belmont promised her that they would avenge him, but that didn't seem to bring her any comfort. She became the saddest person I've ever seen. Her chin never left her chest. The man who stabbed Jawbone injured two other people who were nowhere near his knife. In Morne Jaloux, people died all the time, but none as young as Jawbone. His passing left a gloom over that place on the hill.

Two days after Jawbone's funeral, Goday vanished. We looked for him everywhere, at his grandmother's house down in Belmont, in Springs where we both knew some people. Finally, my father suggested we use the dogs. They took some of his dirty clothes and waved them in the nose of two hunting dogs. The animals took off across the cane, sniffed around for a while and eventually they led my father and the others men to a cave deep in the trees. Inside they found Goday sitting quietly.

My father told us that night he knew exactly what happened to Goday. It had to have been a Ladablais, the imp who appear like a beautiful woman but had one cow foot. They frequently lured young boys into the woods and use them for vile purposes. But I knew no Ladablais tricked Goday. He was way too smart for that.

That was the first time I doubted my father. I didn't say it loud, but I knew something had crept between us. The sensation reminded me of glimpsing an object just before it fades and you know it's gone forever. From that day on, I knew I would question his every word. I realized then that no demon killed Jawbone; another man wielding a knife murdered him. Everything became very stark to me.

Goday started skipping school; spending many nights hunting the woods beyond the cane with his two dogs. When the time came for us to sit our final exams, Goday didn't even show up. I made a perfect score and received a scholarship. The day before I left Grenada for the University of the West Indies in Jamaica, ten years ago. I went to Goday's house to say goodbye. Miss Idona told me he'd just left with his dogs and might not be back for days.

No one met me at the airport. I should have expected that because I told no one I was coming. The taxi driver was a talkative fellow. He kept talking about a new political party called the Jewell Movement. I showed no interest in the politic of Grenada and the fellow grew tired of me. We drove in silence. I was trying to make out how things had progressed. It seemed to me not much had changed in ten years.

At the house, I was greeted like the Prodigal Son. Enid hugged me for the first time. My two younger brothers looked grown, young men. We shook hands. Enid lowered her voice. "So good to see you, Cammy. He'll be glad you're home. That stroke robber him of so much," and she broke into tears.

His appearance was shocking. I had never seen my father on his back before. The man was pale and withered, folded in white sheets, his eyes wide and watery, struggling to verbalize.

I couldn't help but wonder if my presence was causing him pain. His attempt to speak almost brought tears to my eyes. Spittle was easing out of one edge of his lip. I wiped his mouth with the corner of the sheet and he grasped my hand. His fingers were cold and shaking. I knew there had to be words swelling up in his chest, trying to escape. Enid stuck her head in the door after about ten minutes and told me Goday was outside. I was relieved.

Except for a few scars on his face and forehead, Goday looked good in the twilight. Young and strapping, he reminded me of his father.

"How you doing brother. It's nice to see you," and he threw his arms around me. Enid told me you doing good in the States." He pushed me out to arms length and looked at me before he released me and stepped back.

Wet Storage and Other Stories

I felt awkward and embarrassed as if I had somehow betrayed him.

"How's life, Goday?"

"I'm treating life well. I just survived my first strike. The cane workers walked out of the fields and it lasted for a whole month. Everyone was after me, including some of the same people I was trying to help."

"You mixed up with trouble makers huh?" I said.

Goday smiled and cocked his head to one side. I looked at him and I felt jealous. In that instant, I knew there was more to him than I could ever muster, even with my education, my credit cards and all my money in the bank. It reminded me of that evening after the fight with Stumpy, the way I felt after he had instructed me in the tactics of fighting.

"You can call it that," he said. "We had lots of help from the new political party, the Jewell Movement. Cammy, which is more important capital or labor?"

The question came at me from an oblique angle, totally unexpected. "I would say they are equally important."

Goday looked at me and smiled. "We have a lot to talk about, Cammy. I'll borrow my girl's car and come get you tomorrow. I want you to meet some people. Go see your father."

I turned toward the house, returning to my sick father, silently hoping that all this would end for him soon.

MUMBO JUMBO

Three days had passed since we buried Karol Lagrenade under the mango tree near his grandmother's house. Now his mother, Anna stood in our yard holding her younger son, Ian, by one hand. She held a basket covered with a clean towel in the other. I knew the basket was full of bread. Ian looked as though he might pull away and bolt. His head was moving back and forth, but his bandy legs remained planted firmly on the ground. My father went outside and spoke to Anna. He came back and told me we are going to see an old lady up in Jan Anglais.

We went to the home of an old woman who lived off the main road in a wooden house. The place was nestled in a grove of fruit trees. She had mangoes, sapodillas, oranges, and ugly fruits, all laden and ripe. I wanted to ask her for some of her fruits; Ian and I could have had a good time with some of those. But everybody looked so serious, even that pretty girl, the one the old woman called Alma.

We sat in a small room in the old woman's house. She was fair skinned, and short. Her head was wrapped in a piece of plain cloth. She had eyes like a snake's, and the fingers on her hands resembled those of a child. Still, the old woman's overall appearance reminded me of an old tree.

The room was cramped. We sat touching each other. A small red and white statue of the Virgin Mary rested on a shelf near a bouquet of dead flowers. One candle balanced in the right hand of the figurine. Dozens of vials in different sizes containing dried whole leaves adorned every shelf in the room. Alma brought a basin with clean water and a white towel. She placed the container on the old woman lap, and then she left.

The room emitted many sharp smells, herbs, candle-smoke, nameless essences that boiled down to tenfold questions running around in my head.

The old woman sprinkled a powder on the surface of the water, and the stuff dissipated across the top of the liquid. She placed her hands in the water, brought them out, and then rested them on the towel.

An odor rose out of the basin disguised, sweet-scented in my nose, but my eyes watered. I looked at Ian; he was rigid, nothing moved. Not even his head or shoulders. His mother still held his hand and was speaking as the old woman finished with the white towel and tossed it to the floor, near where she had placed the basin.

"Mama, I lost my son, I lost my first born. What's happening to me? Tell me Mama, my children." Mize Anna looked as if she might start bawling, the way she did the morning they pulled Karol's body out of the sea.

"I heard about your troubles, Anna. I wish this were easy for you. This World is not our home, we all just passing through. Your son left his marks everywhere. If you came to me before, I could have tried to prevent some of your pain, but now . . . I can't turn that back. I'm sorry Anna. I keep seeing this man with blood on his hands, just standing there. I can't see his face though. That vessel is in the way. Did they name the vessel DELPHINE?"

The old woman paused and looked around the room. She studied our faces as if our expressions could tell her something or take her to the place where she wanted to go. When she spoke next, she spoke to Anna and my father as if dealing with one person.

"You brought these boys here for obvious reasons. Let me see your hands, Ian . . . "

The old woman opened her palms and presented them to Ian. He hesitated and his mother bumped him with her elbow. Ian's hands flew out, trembling. He placed them in Mama Viche's. The old woman took a deep breath, and then the air came flying back through her mouth as if someone slapped her on her back. She spoke to Anna as she caught her breath.

"Oh lord! Anna, this boy will help take Grenada apart and put it back together again." She laughed out loud as if someone told her an excellent joke. "Don't worry about him, Anna. He'll be fine. The spirits are real strong in him. Just mourn your lost child. Don't worry about this one." Ian glanced up at his mother as the old woman finished speaking, a smile barely visible at the corners of his mouth. I knew that look. It was relief.

Mama Viche licked her lips with a pink tongue, then she turned to me sitting near my father, and my heart trembled. I saw something on her face, in her eyes, something solid. My eyes blinked rapidly the moment she spoke my name.

"Godfrey," she said, "your father doesn't believe in any of this Mumbo Jumbo. He brought you here because Anna is his friend and he needs to put her heart at ease." She smiled and shrugged her shoulders. "Give me your hands anyway," she said to me.

I hesitated but then I remembered Ian's reaction. I didn't want to look foolish or coward, so I leaned forward and place my hands in her palms, hoping for nothing. She gently folded smooth, cold fingers over my hands and I felt a sensation, like the tingle I felt the time I touched the two poles of that flat rectangular transistor battery to my tongue.

I looked deep into the old woman's eyes this time and my skin shivered. She was looking into me as I was looking into her. The whole thing reminded me of gazing into a mirror that reflected into another mirror. I tried to disconnect from her glare, but I was wedged there. And her first few words sounded like she was sweet-talking me.

"Godfrey, do you know it's possible to call things by name and still not recognize them? For instance, your father calls what we doing here Mumbo Jumbo. That's the name of our protection spirit. It followed us all the way from Africa to this world. The white people know its name. They printed it in that big book of captured words. Your father calls that spirit by name and he doesn't know it. You're filled with that spirit, but it's hidden, like water below ground. You know some people see you as mud. Boy? A, that's all they can see. You hidden within some old tones, music knows your name--

"But pay attention, you will come across five Ehis, spirits wearing skin. They will teach you and you will find out many things. Near the end of your journey, you will be presented with a beautiful gift, but you will have to leave that behind and travel again, alone. Tell me about your dreams, Godfrey. What you notice when you walk in the spirit world? You ever told your father about the Snipes you see dancing around his shadow in the water?" She hesitated. "It doesn't matter," she said softly, "what will be, will be."

Her steady gaze wilted to sadness and she shook her head slowly. In the mean time, I attempted to focus my thoughts, tried to put my dreams into words; they refused to take form. I decided to speak any words before my anxieties drown me. Something like a lie, but not quite, came out of my mouth.

"I can't remember dreams when I'm awake, Mama?" I said.

The words came out of my mouth and they surprised me. The old woman released my hands, and pulled back. A mixture of surprise and amusement covered her face. I had a feeling that she understood what I said more than I did, and that troubled me. I was hoping she wouldn't sum up or force me to go into some excruciating explanation about my statement.

"Well, you maintaining the vow. Refusing to interfere, huh. Remember Godfrey; the cutlass cuts only one ways. We all must earn our scars. If you ever need me, I'll be here."

Wet Storage and Other Stories

She turned away from me and faced Anna, "Anna, thank you for the bread," she continued. "Ethan Soulages, bring me two pounds of fish the next time you have a good catch. And will you gut them for me. Alma is kind of squirmy about touching the innards. The fate of your son is in his own hands, Ethan. Keep his feet on the ground. That's all you can do." My father was nodding his head as the old woman spoke. She dug into her pocket. "Take these." She handed one vial to my father and another to Anna. "Crush them in warm water. Man Better Man, that's all it is. Don't let them drink it. Let them take sponge baths with it for thirty days, every night before bed. And these, Ian And Godfrey, wear them around your waist. Wear them all the time." she handed one little leather pouch attached to a string to each of us.

The meeting ended; I felt as if I had caused this unceremonious conclusion by not telling the old woman about my dreams. But what could I tell her? My dreams were far too filigreed for words. On the way back home, Ian and I walked far behind our parents. Long skinny shadows danced on the ground near our feet. I wanted to make sense of all the things the old woman had said.

"What did she mean when she said you would take Grenada apart and put it back together?" I asked Ian.

"Who knows anything about all that Obeah? I like that Mumbo Jumbo though. It's always nice to have a guardian. But what's those Ehis for you. What's an Ehi? Spirits with skin?" He giggled nervously. "That stuff she sprinkled in the water smelled familiar." He paused and went silent as we came closer to our parents.

I placed little stock in what the old woman had said. I knew spirits. They hid off the road in bushes. They flew across the night as balls of fire, they wail and cry, scaring the hell out man and beast. But none of them have skin. If spirits had skins someone would have found one already, just like they find snakeskins, and bring them home to use in no-good spells. No one has ever seen a spirit skin as far as I know. So, what is she talking about?

I had some ideas about where I stood in this world. I could make no sense of Mama Viche's tidings. Not for Ian or anyone else. Not with words. I knew I was blessed. I knew that Mother Earth, or whatever spirits that rule this realm; they had some plans for me. But to whom could I tell this? These people would think I was stone crazy or stuck-up, and that was the last thing I needed.

I wore Mama Viche's little pouch around my waist for many years. By now, I had traveled to the United States and was playing soccer at a school in Portland, Maine. Some of my teammates grew curious about the pouch and started asking questions. I decided the story would be too long to tell. So, I hid the pouch in a draw. It was a dreary day in North America on my twenty-first birthday. I was standing looking out of the window of a small apartment. A little wet bird was sitting in the branches of a denuded tree. Why are you still here? Why don't you fly south? The bird could have been thinking the same thoughts about me.

The desire to see what might be inside the pouch overwhelmed me. I cut the thread sewn around the edge of the leather and inside I found a piece of paper folded in plastic. Carefully, I unfolded the paper. The words in very small script began: The Lord is my shepherd.

WALKING IN MEMPHIS

My tenth birthday fell on the same Saturday that my mother took me to Memphis. We traveled by bus, to see my father and the zoo at Overton Park. They kept all the animals in cages. I felt strange, standing there, looking into the eyes of the primates. They seemed so human. I never forgot those cages, the stink, and the sad looks in the eyes of the animals as they paced and bawled from beyond the steel bars and concrete. It never occurred to me that just fourteen years later I would be caged.

These cells form an echo chamber. The screams, the tears at night, the confessions to a God that had already turned his back, all that is here, locked in, no breeze to push the stench through. No sleeping here. Why waste life on sleep? There will be lots of time to sleep after death. I'm the silent one in this place. No begging, no pleading. I'll give them no such satisfaction.

In the years that I've been here, politics have become my tools. I like to consider myself a political prisoner, but some may disagree. When you are subjected to a bureaucracy whose language is politics and legalese, you learn those tongues quickly. So, if you think I'm engaging in polemics, shouting from the proverbial soapbox, you are correct. It's all I have left, this constant argument striving to shape and reshape a reality to justify my existence.

They locked me in here around the time that Ronald Regan was President. He came and went. George Bush came and went. Bill Clinton took office. No pardon for me on Bill's last day. Each year they threaten me with death, over twenty years of repeated threats. I would call that cruel and unusual. If you want to kill a man, stake him out and put a bullet in his head.

This threat has shadowed me all my life. Its possible fulfillment offers a mixed relief, a kind of euphoria that hits my brain, and makes it careen. This terrific confusion is like an opiate. It's a form of self-defense, self-preservation; the same beast that landed me in this fix.

I bought a revolver and started packing it around. What can I say about that? I did not intend to die like my father. So, I have only one regret, that they managed to capture me. All I can say in that regard, I'm alive for the time being, and the man who tried to kill me is dead. It took me many years in this stinking hole to recognize my place in the struggle.

Genocide, that's all the shit is. Cull the alpha males. Must be a secret plan somewhere in the bowels of this wretched nation. Why else would so many black men be imprisoned or killed daily. All those twisted believers, ignorant racists, angry black brothers, marauding policemen, and me, fair game for all of them.

The truth is I was more likely to be the victim rather than the perpetrator of any crime. So many mothers' sons. Poor people's children. Oh, some of us manage to avoid the traps; they are many ways to do that. Education is only one of them. I had that opportunity and blew it in the classic fashion, so I'm not looking for sympathy here. I'm just laying it down, trying to let you see this from my view, from the perspective of meditation on eminent death. No one kills one of those bastards and live to tell the tale to his grandchildren.

What was the first step? Hard to recall. I remember some vague turning points, but only in hindsight. Repeatedly, trying to relive one split second as if that could make a difference. I made that decision, and it was done. Just like that. There stood reality, naked and pornographic. The man slumped, blood leaking through the holes in his clothes. Everything was so ambiguous, except the small puddle gathering on the ground near the seat of his pants. A mixture of fluids, diluting the red of his blood. I stood there and watched.

My last day of freedom was over twenty years ago. The world I remember is long gone. Let's see if I can sum it up for you. The day began in the basement of a morgue. It began badly and grew worst. The whole thing started in that mortician's card game. There was that strange, anxious silence. I remember it now in a curious particular way, especially how the morning light filtered through the tattered material covering the only window high on the yellow concrete wall. The repetitious clicking of the plastic poker chips hardly disturbed the stillness.

No one glued my backside to the chair that morning, but it felt that way. A kind of weight held me down. Around the poker table sat eight men, slowly fondling their piles of green chips. The chairs and the table, the small avocado-green refrigerator and another table with a coffee maker, these things filled a small subterranean room below the main floor of the mortuary. An ache in my backside inched down my legs.

A coarse fire shot down my calves and settled in my heels. I wiggled my toes, drew my legs in, and took a deep breath. I caught the familiar scent of lily talcum, formaldehyde and tobacco smoke, the dominant aromas of these gatherings and something else. Nothing as obvious as the stink of their anxious sweat or their sly beer farts. Something less palpable seems to linger in the air that morning. It took me this long to recognize it, but I know what it is now. Bodies exude a certain scent when frightened or anxious. That stench is merciless around these cells.

Although I had sat in that room, at those games often, I still could not shake the idea of dead bodies upstairs. When I die, would they bring my body back there? Will there still be guys in the basement, chasing the same dollars, lying to each other? Will they care that my dead body was upstairs? Would they bring me down, prop me up at my favorite seat and deal me a royal flush?

The silence was broken. The numbness in my legs prevented me from focusing on the action of the cards. Nevertheless, the smooth tone of the mortician's voice threw me into a rage. Irwin, the mortician, was doing his usual thing, and I listened with mounting disgust. I was near broke and listening to his attempt to justify his rake had a smarmy feel. I frowned and shook my head. Irwin was playing nicey-nicey to a young college fellow called Billy, enticing him to remain in the game instead of cashing his gains. The mortician swiveled his head on his fat neck, glanced at me quickly. The big mole near his nose twitched. He ran his tongue over his lips and used my full names in his next sentence, but I knew he was still aiming his comments at Billy.

"Johnny Brazil, what you shaking your head for? I must pay the cops. It's all greasing the palms. That's how it works. For instance in my funeral business, even the preachers are there with their hands out," he said. "They are always hovering around the house, before and after a death. All of them have my card. They whisper a few words in the ears of the bereaved. If the work happens to come my way, I'm in church the next Sunday with a fat envelope for that man of the cloth. That's the way it is. Irwin laughed with just his mouth. His eyes remained fixed on the action of the bet and the quick hands of the dealer pitching the cards and raking the proper percentage of the pot.

I flung my cards to the dealer. Enough. I stood up, stretched, and the circulation rushed down my legs like a thousand little needles. I repositioned the gun under my old brown jacket and left without saying a word. As usual, I climbed some steep stairs to a concrete walkway that lead to the alley behind the mortuary. The alley was long and narrow, lined with garbage cans and stray dogs. November morning in Memphis. Much too cold for the mid-south. My size twelve's displaced the gravel as I moved down the alley.

Looking back, I now see that alley as one of those turning points. That was the very place where those three bastards came at me. I've always wondered why they chose me, because I'm not a small man; less than two years ago I was a star basketball player, but they came at me fast, with intent. Wolves attacking a straggler. I knocked one of them down and the other two jumped me. The one I had knocked down came back at me with a blade. I thought I was dead. I woke up with gravel in the skin of my face, some missing teeth, two nasty flesh wounds and my wallet gone. That's when I decided to buy a gun. Never again would I be caught off guard. Never again would I be subjected to such humiliation.

Although I hated daylight, I grudgingly welcomed the warmth of the sun on my back that morning. I felt drained, but not tired. That sluggish feeling always came over me after losing at poker. I wished somehow I could just banish all my worries. I knew that in the not too long, my girlfriend, Ethel, would tell me to hit the road. The house belonged to her, she paid all the bills, and I've been staying out all night much too often. So, I planned to avoid her that morning.

What a fucking life. Whatever happened to the days of wine, good food, cheers from fresh-faced girls? Whatever happened to that keen steady focus? Just one false move and bam, busted. That pudgy white face of the dean of students, using words like examples, standards of behavior and moral conduct. He would stop and look at me after each declaration as if savoring the moment. Each word issued from his mouth seemed to lower me into a hole. Each time he broke his silence felt like shovels of dirt falling on my coffin. The son of a bitch sounded as if he had caught me screwing his wife. If I looked more like him, would he have chosen to be more lenient? They were waiting with all their preconceived notions. I told you those niggers are no good. We should never have allowed them close to our school. Lots of good decent white boys can play basketball.

All of that was coursing through my brain that morning as I moved down that alley, passing toppled garbage cans with stray dogs glancing at me as if I might be competition for the refuse. Those old rancid thoughts.

I lasted two years at the university, along with Buddy Weeks, my old friend. We learned more than the books had to teach. I allowed myself to go astray. Buddy came up with an idea to make some quick cash. Start with the jocks. Form a pool, bet on the weather, skim a little now and then—an administrative fee. No sports betting.

The game went like this. At first, the bet was two dollars, then it changed to five. The action was good. All players deposited the bet, and then we made a call to obtain the weather prediction from the National Weather Service, daily at eight in the morning. The object was to use their prediction as a basis. If the weather service was right, no one won and we required another five to continue in the game. Everyone between two degrees above or two degrees below the actual temperature inside the metro area was paid some of the pot. Those at one degree below or above shared the pot, or won it outright in the case of a single person guessing right.

They won the first few pools easily. Money changed hands with little fanfares, but one pool turned into a monster. The National Weather Service kept predicting the correct temperature. The pool hit a thousand dollars, the campus came alive, and the stampede headed straight to Buddy's and my door.

It took eight more days to arrive at the determining night. The weather service predicted twenty-five degrees. I thought that would be too low. I felt more confident with thirty degrees but didn't predict thirty, instead I predicted twenty-eight. I had reasoned that if it turned out to be twenty-six degrees I would be off by two points. And if the weather service turned out to be right again, I would be off by only three points—a kind of victory. I was hoping that the others would guess much higher, and the pool would continue to grow. All that cash and Buddy and me retaining twenty percent.

The actual temperature turned out to be twenty-nine degrees at eight o'clock that morning. I won the big pool and the grumbling started. The investigation by campus security took two weeks. They concluded that Buddy and I were the ringleaders in a gambling scheme. They expelled both of us. I hadn't seen Buddy Weeks in two months, and didn't care to see him. The last I heard of Buddy, he was arrested for poking sponges up the nostrils of racehorses. Man still trying to get paid the easy way.

I came out of the alley and out of my contemplation on things gone bye. I stood and looked both ways down McLemore Avenue. Another Saturday morning in Memphis. I turned west, heading toward the Mississippi River. My eyes darted here and there as cars and people poured by me like liquid. Two policemen stared me down from their black and white cruiser moving slowly in the opposite direction. The cops reminded me of scenes from those old movies of the Gestapo searching for froward Jews in Nazi occupied lands.

I tucked my hands into my pockets and crouched down, attempting to look ordinary. Hard to do when you

Wet Storage and Other Stories

are six feet two inches tall and over two hundred pounds. Don't come after me; please don't come after me. If they find this gun, I'll be in jail for sure and I have enough troubles already.

The car kept moving and I was thankful. I thought of my mother and I knew I would never find the courage to tell her they expelled me? Graduation was only two months away. Sorry Mom, I gambled your hard earned money away, every penny you sent me, can't fulfill that dream for you. The first college-educated person in our family.

I walked with that weight on my shoulders. Dyersburg, the place where I was born, just four hours away; I hadn't been home in six months. This city, these games were killing me fast, just like my father before me. He came here with his guitar, looking for Beal Street, Stax Records, money and fame. Poor son of a bitch.

I needed to give Ethel more time to be out of the house. I couldn't face her that morning. What a night. Things would be better after a good sleep and sometime to figure out a strategy. I had talked her out of kicking me to the curb before.

I blamed everyone and everything for my stagnant luck. Even the advancing sunshine became an enemy that day. I longed for the shrouded sanctuary of night, which allowed me to live anonymously in this crowded distant place; hide my shame. What a wasted night. I frequently endured those pangs of guilt and self doubt after games that lasted long after sunrise. The crisp ten in my pocket did not ease my self-recrimination. For all intent and purposes, I was broke.

C. C. Alick

I'd planned to win at least a hundred dollars that night, but that fellow called Billy had made a whole parcel of foolish bets, and got lucky each time. Asshole with an asshole kind of name. What kind of name is Billy for a black man? Billy Dee, Billy Eckstine, Billie Holiday even, but not plain Billy. Sounds like a white boy from Kansas. I spat to clear the spoiled taste from my mouth. The spit splayed out star shaped on the concrete pavement. The old gambling ballad "Stagilee" came to mind as I made my way across Main Street and turned south toward Riverside Drive.

I skirted MLK park, named after another black man cut down in the prime of his life. Sons of bitches still culling all the alpha males out of the black population. The giant Poplars stood guard around the fringes of the woods. I didn't enter; I kept moving through the neighborhood that I knew would take me to South Parkway. This part of Memphis, near the interstate, was home to many poor black souls from all over the Midsouth, Tunica, Mississippi, the farm country beyond West Memphis Arkansas. Migrants to the city looking for work. So many of them chose to remain here. Why not move on up the river to places like, Cincinnati, Chicago or Indianapolis? Or why not be a true adventurer and follow the Big Muddy to her place of birth in the deep woods of Minnesota.

My father chose to come here, to this city on the banks of the Mississippi river where he found only death. He died around my thirteenth birthday. Shot down by a couple of plain-clothes cops who thought they had stumbled on an armed robbery. When they sent his body home, he was still clutching his guitar. We thought of breaking his fingers to get the instrument out of his hand, but instead we buried him with it. I often wonder if anyone in Memphis remembers the man called Theodore Brazil. I searched every issue of the Commercial Appeal for the year the cops killed my father; he was not mentioned.

I need to get off the street just in case those two cops decided to make a big circle. Didn't need the harassment. I knew just the place in that neighborhood where I could waste an hour or so. Kill two birds with one stone as the cliché goes. Give Ethel a little more time to leave the house.

I moved across a parking lot strewn with shards of broken glass—green, brown, clear; the cigarette butts and empty packets adorned the asphalt, all fetching the rays of the sun like baubles. I looked up at the busted neon sign hanging over the door. The only visible symbols on the sign read C86LBY, spread haphazard across shattered white plastic. A stupid name for a bar. The place was familiar to me, but I hadn't haunted these digs in almost a year. Buddy and I came down here frequently in the old days.

I walked through a heavy wooden door and hesitated at the entrance, scrutinizing the room. Red neon dissected the dark. Silhouettes decayed and languished across empty tables and chairs. No one saw me standing at the door. No one turned to look at me. I was thankful. Nine o'clock on a Saturday, and already.

For just a second I thought of turning away, but the music oozing from the jukebox in the far corner beguiled me. It was a drippy piece of jazz, laced with strings, reminded me of rain and the kind of music piped into grocery stores. I recognized it as Ahmad's Blues—

C. C. Alick

Ahmad Jamal subtlety pecking the keys on the piano. Instead of filling the room, the music barely reached the door, enticing me to enter.

Eight hard cores sat at the long, dimly lit counter. Poor suckers. I recognized the bartender, a tall thin West Indian fellow who moved like a dancer. Everyone called him Tobago, after the island his father came from. He moved amongst the half-empty bottles of booze and well-drained glasses, cleaning up from the night before. The man was a bad ass, they say. He killed a fellow that pulled a gun on him. He did some time. I remained at the entrance surveying the bar. A man in the far corner was shaving.

I eyed the entire room, and returned to the person in the corner. The man was dipping his finger into his glass from time to time and rubbing his face. The other patrons sat crouched over their drinks in silence. I recognized a few of the faces as I moved onto the floor, and took off my jacket. I slid the gun into the pocket and found a seat at the bar, allowing ample space between the other patrons and me. Tobago was now speaking to the shaving man at the far end.

"Stop that shit before you slit your own throat, man. Nothing's worth that . . . You know what I mean?" He spoke with a cordial accent. His last words sounded like some kind of punctuation—you know what I mean. He moved toward me as he spoke. He barely took his eyes off the man in the corner.

"A man can't even get a plain shave in this place. We should burn this fucker down," the shaving man said.

I knew that voice. He sounded as if grumbling, but you could hear him across the entire room.

"This is not a barbershop. This is a bar," Tobago said.

"Could have fooled me," said the shaving man.

I glanced down the bar. The familiar gaunt man wearing a dirty white shirt sat with a tumbler full of whisky before him. He was dipping one finger into the whisky, smearing it on his cheeks, and shaving the skin with a pearl handle straight razor. The harmless spite I had carried into the bar drained away, replaced by an explicitly more ominous sense of dread.

Buddy Weeks was foul when drunk, and unpredictable. I bemoaned my pathetic financial condition, and was rueful of the two hundred dollars I had borrowed from him to remain in the poker game two months before. Buddy's hand froze in mid motion as our eyes met, the razor poised on his right cheek. He then brought the razor slowly down to the counter and swirled it gingerly in his whiskey. Without shifting his eyes off me, he snatched for the glass, emptied the contents into his mouth, then he slammed the glass down on the counter. Not one patron flinched.

"Tobago, bring me another double; that clown is paying," he called down the bar, pointing at me.

I smiled reluctantly and threw my last ten on the bar.

"How's it going, Buddy? ... Get him one; I'll have a Gilbeys on the rocks."

The familiar stink of tobacco, liquor, and unwashed bodies hit my face. My heart pounded. I became aware of cool moisture inside my shirt. I decided in one instant to stand my ground. Face this. No more ducking, hiding. I felt a sensation, something akin to the tingles I experience while placing fragile bets.

"Told you I would have your money the first of the month," I replied.

"That was last month. The month before you said the same thing. I'll bet even your cheap ass isn't worth a buck a pound."

"I had your money last month, but you were in jail . . . for something with horses. This shit isn't necessary, man."

"I'll say what's fucking necessary. You knew where I was . . . Could have visited, brought me a packet of cigarettes."

The bartender placed a drink before me, then started to carry the other down the bar to Buddy.

"No! Tobago, I'll take that right there. Place it next to my compadre," Buddy pointed at me. "We old friends, you know. Played basketball together. Went to school together. Got expelled for gambling together." Buddy chuckled. The words left his lips like stones thrown.

"I remember," Tobago said.

He hesitated with the drink in hand. He measured Buddy and me like a referee, then placed the drink on the bar before the stool next to mine. Buddy clutched his razor and commenced to stagger down the bar. I thought of the gun in my jacket pocket. I thought of taking it out and placing it on the bar. After all, he had a weapon in hand. However, I decided against that. Tobago looked at me as if attempting to convey a signal. Every instinct told me to leave the drink, run for the door, but my feet refused to move. Tobago raised his brows and shrugged his shoulders. Buddy piled into the stool next to me, still holding the razor in hand. His eyes were blood red and sketchy, his face like rumpled cloth. I sat, waited.

"Put that thing away, man. I don't feel like inviting the cops to this party today. Okay?" Tobago spoke and moved away to another customer. His easy admonition to Buddy sounded calm, sociable. Kind of ordinary. I felt hopeful.

"The cops! Ha! Ha!" Buddy waved his hand with the razor in the air, an indignant look smeared all over his wrinkled face. The laughter came out of his mouth like venom. "I could skin all of you before they get here, post your asses to God. The cops don't give one shit about a bunch of butt nuggets like you. The more of you in the grave the better off they feel. Make their jobs easier." He flung the razor on the bar, snatched at his drink, and took a long swig.

I thought I could ease the tension by speaking, but the word that came out of my mouth sound dumb even before they hit the air.

"Isn't there some ban against spouting politics or religion in a bar," I said?

"Dumb ass rule . . . And who the fuck asked you?"

Buddy sprung off the stool, stood with his legs apart, both hands thrown up as if ready to fight. His eyes blazed, his face looked damp and nervy, globs of spittle collected at the far corners of his lips. He rocked back and forth.

I faced Buddy but remained seated. I took my eyes off him for an instant and glanced at the razor on the bar, regretting that action immediately. Buddy's eyes followed mine straight to the razor. I thought of making a grab for it, like gunslingers reaching for the pistol on the bar. Reach for it; pick it up, you yellowbelly . . .

"You owe me two hundred dollars. I want it right now. You rat fuck piece of shit."

A scatter of spittle flew out of Buddy's mouth with the last word. I casually ran my hand over my face and gestured at the bar. I struggled to keep my mind off the gun.

"That change is my last money, Buddy. I'm being upright with you, man."

I stood up, stuffed both hands into my pockets, and brought the white insides out. They hung down the sides of my pants like a dog's droopy ears. Buddy reached out, took one empty pocket in hand, held it firm, snatched the razor from the bar, and with one swipe severed the pocket from my pants. I snapped back like a taut rubber band.

"You crazy son of a bitch! You nearly cut me! ... Two years, man, almost two years and you still blaming me." I inched toward my coat hanging on the back of the chair.

"Okay, okay you two, cut that shit right now," Tobago shouted. He stared at Buddy and me from across the bar.

"We cool . . . we done for now," Buddy spoke without shifting his eyes off me.

"It was your idea, Buddy. You said the university wouldn't care, as long as we stayed away from sports."

"You brought the man down on us, Brazil. You did. We had a good thing going. A way off these streets." He threw the severed pocket at me. "You owed me two hundred bucks, right . . ." he continued, "Now you owe me one. Consider that a discount. I'm not through with you yet. Have the rest of my money the next time I see you. You hear me?"

Buddy folded the razor and stuffed it into his pocket. He reached for his drink and emptied the remainder into his mouth. All this seemed to take forever. He placed the glass on the counter, and without looking back at me, he headed for the front door.

I looked at Tobago and at my severed pocket. I tried to smile, but my face felt like stone. Tobago turned away. With Buddy gone, a little of my former animosity returned. I told myself that blood and money were the same things. Just different forms of currency. I was sure that little difference existed between a man that sold his blood for money and a man that sold the hours of his life for money. I wondered if Buddy now waited outside the front door, what would be his choice? Kill me or maim me? I decided to bait the odds.

It became clear to me that all of that was another game. Figure the odds. I had no intentions of walking into anything blind, not anymore, especially something that could result in death. I looked around the bar and found what I was looking for. Another way out.

I took my jacket off the back of the chair, removed the gun from the pocket, snuggled it in my right palm and threw the jacket over it. I left the last of my drink on the bar, pocketed my change, and headed for the back door. The phone rang as I reached the narrow entrance leading down the corridor. Tobago answered the phone, and I imagined the call I would have to make to my mother.

The way she would speak the moment she recognized my voice. Johnny! It's you! What you doing, baby?

School going good? ... I have a little problem, Mom, I imagined myself saying. They threw me out of school. I knew I would have to use those words or something very similar. Talk to them, son. They will understand. That's what she would say. However, I knew that meant begging and I swear never to go down on my knees for any motherfucker. Especially for people who would enjoy seeing you beg, receive all their joy from your humiliation and still say no.

The back door flapped open as I reached midway down the hallway. A glare filled the entrance blinding me, but I got a glimpse of a white shirt. My palm tightened around the grip of the gun, my finger snuggled on the trigger, my heart pounded in my chest. I threw my back against the wall as the door swung, shutting out the light; a stranger slipped by barely glancing at me. I looked around the corridor and marveled at how close I came to firing. I stood there for a moment, then I ran and hit the door. The door flew opened, and I dashed outside.

I saw them just before the bullet struck the wood near my face. Buddy was just a little down the alley. The cop was Moving away from his car with his gun drawn, motioning and shouting at Buddy. When I rushed through the door, the cop turned and fired. Now he was standing between Buddy and me, looking back and forth as if assessing which one of us to kill first.

He moved with the gun pointed, repositioning himself for a better shot at me. That's when I fired the gun, over and over, from beneath the jacket. At first, I doubted whether I had hit him at all, but then the results became obvious. I saw Buddy scale a fence, heard a dog barking. I stood there looking at the man and my feet refused to move, but voices inside my head began shouting run, run, run.

REDEMPTION SONGS

I'm not a talkative person. So, some might conclude that I'm stupid. I learned a long time ago that it's good to listen. You learn many things if you keep your mouth shut and your eyes and ears open. Act like a fly on the wall and behold the universe come talking to you in more ways than you care to understand.

You are familiar with the repeating dreams that some people constantly endure? In my dream there's someone or something chasing me. I would escape every time by flying away. I never looked back at my pursuer for quite a long time. One night I did look back. And there stood the figure of a man. I had never set eyes on him before that night in the dream, but I knew him. His name was Nails Gittens, my grandfather.

One day I heard my aunt Velma complaining. She said the good men were afraid to come around because of Nails. I was twelve years old at the time and Nails had been dead for just as long, but for some reason he remained. Every time I heard the platitude hard as nails, I knew they were referring to him. Nails abided with all of us, my uncle, my four aunts, and me. I'm unsure about so much. Certainties move so strangely. Some things that you assume to be facts today might not remain so tomorrow.

Take for instance the circumstances of my birth. A man twice my mother's age seduced and impregnated her. She was fifteen years old at the time. Her father, Nails, found out and invited the man to go hunting. It took the police a long time to find the body of the man who would have been my father. A fellow called Vince Malotte. They arrested my grandfather, and after a long sensational trial, where he steadfastly declared his innocence, he was found guilty, and taken to the prison at Richmond Hill. The prison authority did exactly what the judge ordered. They hanged him by the neck until he was dead. His youngest child, my uncle Flyn, was just five years old at the time.

No one shielded me from this. In the condescending ways of adults, they had no idea I was listening. The account came to me in little pieces, whispers, jokes and sly remarks, about the hangman and the house full of women. I grew up regularly gathering and fitting pieces together, afraid to ask any final questions. I'm thankful now, that no one fed me this as one meal. It would have been too big to swallow in one sitting. The little bites were bad enough. They left some bitter tastes at the back of my throat every time I digested one of them.

After I had amassed the heap, and placed the oddments in a reasonable line, things started to clear up for me. Like why my grandmother treated me differently from all her other grandchildren and why she never mentioned the name of her daughter who gave birth to me. She always refers to her as that girl in Trinidad. Even after my grandmother suffered the stroke, and all of us stood around her bed as she lay drooling on the pillow in the room that stunk of camphor. I saw something in those big cow eyes of hers. The stroke had robbed her of her speech, but her eyes held mine like the tentative hugs she at times placed around me.

The motherless child. That was me. The woman who gave birth to me left Grenada for Trinidad when I was four. She never returned and I hardly remember what she looked like. I must have missed her, but I don't recall any anguish. We all called that person Tante Jean. My Aunt Gloria, Tante Jean's sister, she became my mother and raised me as her own. I even carried her husbands' last name. At least that's how they enrolled me in school. I never paid much attention to my surname until I was twenty-two years old and went searching for my birth certificate to emigrate.

I considered using my mother's family name, Gittens, but decided against that, and I knew that Aunt Gloria's name was nothing but a loan. So, I was left with my father's surname, Malotte. It was only after I had written my true name, Whitfield Malotte, that this occurred to me-the tragedy of his life might follow me through that name.

My aunt, Gloria, she thought change might be good for me. Things were going bad enough. My girlfriend had left me for a fellow who was attending the secondary school, and my job was a pain. My boss kept making nasty jokes about natty dread, speaking about my hair as if he had some quarrel with people who wore dreadlocks. Most of my days were spent making all kinds of signs and handbills for the stores around Saint George's, while that greasy, pork-eating lump collected all the money. That was no life. My aunt saw that.

For some years, I had been dabbling with paints and watercolors. I did that for me, and kept them in that little room below aunt Gloria's house. I painted pictures, of things seen in dreams, images suggested by the lift of leaves in the wind. All placed on small pieces of canvas and sometimes paper. I had little cash for materials. I showed one of my portrayals to a woman off of a yacht. It was a depiction of a Jab Jab, a carnival character smeared with charcoal and a mud mask on his face. She got all excited and her husband bought it for her. He paid me fifty dollars. Then they loaned me a magazine with lots of words and pictures about art in the United States. Actually, I never thought of my little drawings as a way of making a living. They were more like a kind of purging. However, after that fellow handed me the money, everything changed.

My aunt saw the magazine, and spotted a big reversed advertisement, you know the ones with the black background and the letters in white. It was for an art school in Miami. So, she put some money together. She made sure I had all my papers looking good, got me a student visa, and dispatched me to Florida to live with her little brother, my uncle Flyn.

Frankly, my aunt just wanted me out of a situation that she presumed could only get worse. She saw the signs of my undoing. So, she posted me off the island, hoping I wouldn't get deported, or voluntarily return to Grenada in six months boasting about my exploits in

America and never leave the island again. We had seen that phenomenon before.

My uncle Flyn was well known. Back home, amongst the Rastas and everybody else who knew him, his nickname was Make-peace. So, it was a big deal when uncle Flyn graduated from law school and went straight to work as a mediator for Dade County, Florida. None of us understood what that meant exactly. He tried to explain his job, but it sounded strange. How can people go to a total stranger with all their problems hanging out of their mouths like dribbles? We didn't understand, so we just laughed. His girlfriend and soon to be wife was looking at us hard. I thought of her as fierce and cruel at the time. Fierce was correct.

The first times I saw them together I was jealous. They came to Grenada and all of our friends and family was sitting around drinking coconut water and gin, rehashing old memories, making jokes. Someone started telling about the time Uncle Flyn had to wear a dress all day because they were washing all his clothes, and my clothes were too small for him. Melba sat, chatting with Aunts, Gloria, Merci, Velma and some other women, but she kept listening to us with one ear. She looked as if she wanted to shoo all of us away from Uncle Flyn, force all of us to treat him with more respect. I had a feeling she had an idea of what it was like for Uncle Flyn and me growing up as the only males in a family of women.

Melba was a Jamaican woman. Her hair, her clothes, she walked, and talked Rastas. She worked as the manager of a Jamaican restaurant owned by her grandmother. Melba and I became great friends on her visits to Grenada. She must have enjoyed seeing Flyn through my eyes.

Above all, I enjoyed listening to her speak about The Pinnacle Community and the man she called brother Howell, an old Rastas prophet who once lived on the run with his followers in the Blue Mountains of Jamaica. I was sure lodging with my uncle Flyn and Melba would be great fun, but that too turned out to be another telling experience.

I landed in Miami in April of Nineteen ninety-two. Three months before my twentieth birthday. That was around the time that a Brinks truck carrying a load of money capsized on an overpass near one of the poorest black neighbors in Miami. The money from the truck rained down onto the street below and people started grabbing. I'll never forget the television showing an old black woman and her grand son walking into the police station with a bag full of money. She reminded me of my grandmother.

The day I arrived, Flynn and Melba met me at the airport, and then we went straight to their house. Melba fed me a dinner of Callaloo with fried fish and boiled green bananas. This surprised me. The food taste exactly like the meals Aunt Gloria cooked back home. Uncle Flyn sat across the table from me depositing food into his mouth, asking questions about his friends and his sisters back home. An electric bulb behind his back shined through his hair. His dreadlocks dangled over his ears. He looked much older than his twenty-five years.

"Gloria said you want to study art," he said. "Is that really what you want?"

C. C. Alick

Melba sat across the table with an empty plate before her. I had the impression that they had discussed this, and she was just looking on now, riding shotgun as they say in the old westerns. She too was looking at me, and waiting.

"I know how to draw pictures," I said.

Flyn smiled. "Whitfield, the first time I saw you draw. You made a circle, put ears and eyes on it. You recall what you did to the mouth?"

I was shaking my head to say no as I swallowed the last bit of buttered callaloo.

"You drew the mouth sewn shut. When I asked you why, you said: Shut-up and listen. I thought you were being fresh, so I boxed your ears. I didn't realize that was the name you gave the picture. We got into our first fight. 'I know how to draw pictures,' he said with a snarl. "You know a lot more than that."

I laughed at what he remembered, because I recalled something like that, yet entirely different. My memories of my uncle Flyn were almost sentimental. He became my hero the day he prevented Zoogoo from beating-up little Punky. Zoogoo was a big bully. We were playing marbles and Punky was winning. Every time he tossed the taw he knocked a mib from the circle. Zoogoo accused Punky of cheating. He balled up his fist and was about to hit Punky, but Flyn stepped between them. Flyn and Zoogoo stared at each other for a long minute, then Flyn spoke softly, "Zoogoo, this is his day. Yours might be tomorrow." Zoogoo could have pushed Flyn out of his way. Nevertheless, he drew back and smiled.

Wet Storage and Other Stories

As we retired that night, Flyn's last words to me should have provided some clues of things to come: "Don't forget to thank Jah for your safe passage, Whitfield," he said.

The next morning was a Saturday. Right after breakfast, Flyn, Melba and me were on our way to a place they called the Sanctuary. Flyn spoke carefully as we wove through traffic; the tone of his conversation carried an irregular sharpness.

"Whitfield, you know Jah never meant for any of us to live as slaves," he said. "Most religions give the impression that we can only achieve redemption through suffering, but Rastafari preaches freedom through the words of Jah and steadfast resistance. Out of bondage. That's what we are about at the Sanctuary."

He glanced back at me as if seeking my reaction. His dreadlocks whipped across his face as he swiveled his neck to look at the road again. Miami looked unbelievable in daylight, a hurricane of noises and foul smells. The air was wet and hot. It was all so coarse, not what I expected.

"We will see Sha Shamane soon, he said. The leader of our church, Elder Kallai Cush, he's in New York right now making arrangements." Flyn glanced at Melba and she smiled, then we sat in silence for a few minutes.

I had heard of the place called Sha Shamane, in Ethiopia, from other Rastas in Grenada. Nevertheless, the way Uncle Flyn was speaking about the place, it bothered me. If they leave for Ethiopia what will I do? Where will I live? His next words answered my questions.

"We want to see Sha Shamane, then we coming back. We'll decide later. See if we want to make it our home. Back to Africa, Whitfield." He glanced back at me again, and smiled through crooked teeth. He sounded as though he was just contemplating a move across town.

A whole host of thoughts bombarded my brain. What are they looking for? All those miles across the world. Sha Shamane or any other spot on the continent of Africa is just another place where people live, and struggle to make a life. I love the belief in Africa, but Africa is within me. However, I kept my mouth shut as the car sped down the road. I didn't want to expose my anxiety and covetousness at the thought of them leaving me behind.

You see, Flyn is my uncle, but he's only five years older than I. He has been more like a big brother instead of an uncle. He introduced me to Ras Tafari when I was twelve, back home. The Rastas tolerated me because of him. I saw the Rastas then as some hairstyles, or maybe a lifestyle, but not as a real religion like the Catholics or the Anglicans. Flyn and Melba's apparent devotion and current approach to Ras Tafari surprised the hell out of me.

I have always known that my birthright was stolen. Hanging with the Rastas in Grenada thought me that. Drawing my pictures was, and still is, an attempt to summon up some of it. I never thought of digesting my loss with God as the water to wash it down. I wanted to come to some kind of understanding of what it means to be an African in the western world.

Wet Storage and Other Stories

My approach has always been basic. God gave me life and must want me to do incredible things with it instead of giving it back. The struggle must go on. That is one of the guiding principles of Rastafari. So listening to Flyn's harangue about some place far across the world sounded like a retreat, a surrender of the faith. After all, slavery did befall us over here; we have a legitimate claim on this land. We did labor and shed blood. Made other people rich. There's no other Promise Land for us. Still, I kept an open mind.

The place they called the Sanctuary was a stucco house on a big corner lot at one hundred Seventy-fifth Street and Eighty-third Avenue. In the Northwest section of Miami. A big wooden sign at the front of the house read: THE ETHIOPIANS ASSEMBLY. At the back of the house was a vegetable garden that looked as if transplanted from Grenada to this big noisy city. They had all kinds of vegetables and greens planted in fine-looking rows. They even kept some small animals, rabbits, and chickens, in coups near two mangoes and a cluster of papaya trees. Three women with two little boys and three little girls were weeding the garden as Flyn and Melba showed me around and introduced me. The adults greeted me cordially, the children waved.

The Rastafarian's Sanctuary turned out to be a square room full of wooden benches and chairs. A few African figures printed on cloth hung here and there. Most of the surrounding walls of the structure were bumpy, low curves and plain buff. In Grenada, the Rastas had no building. We met in the open. On the beach or in the woods, we would cook a big pot of

Manish Water with a goat's head, lots of dumplings, and vegetables we stole from some farmer's garden.

We always listen to reggae music and at sometimes we beat drums. However, after we filled our stomachs, our conversation always turned to the politics, and economics of Grenada. We were more civic than religious.

This Rastafarian church was a new deal for me. I wanted to contribute. I mentioned this to Flyn and Melba, expecting to turn over some of my money, or get invited to some of their meetings. They looked at each other quickly.

"I was hoping you would say something like that," Flyn said. "I'm the treasurer, and I'm also on the committee for the improvement of this temple." He smiled; the word temple came out of his mouth as if referring to some grand cathedral. "You can share your talent, Whitfield. A mural? Stretched along these walls, depicting our history. A couple prophets. Black prophets. Up there." He pointed. "We have a celebration coming up." He smiled again, and continued to gesture toward a pulpit back against the far wall. "What you say? Give me a sketch. I'll show it to Elder Kallai Cush, when he gets back from New York tonight."

I had just arrived. I didn't want to mess with any of that. Things to see and do; preparations for my test. However, uncle Flyn asked me. I was living in his house free, eating his food. I thought seriously, about how I would accomplish what he wanted. This would be the biggest project of my life. After a little contemplation, I was beginning to get the feel of it,

Wet Storage and Other Stories

the idea of it overwhelmed me. Michael Angelo, my Sistine Chapel. It felt good way down in my belly.

I approached it with caution and hope. Flyn spoke and I listened. The vanishing points and the reconciliation of the perspectives came to me easily. I gave Flyn a rough sketch and a list of materials the next day. When the phone on the table at the house rang the same morning, I was reluctant to answer it, but I was the only person in the house and the phone kept ringing. It turned out to be Flyn, calling from the Sanctuary to tell me they loved the design. I could start work anytime.

I needed help to do most of the work, clean the walls of old paint and prep the surface with a good undercoat. Recruiting help was easy. Everybody wanted to be a part of it, along with Flyn and Melba. Elder Kallai Cush and his son, Roots Mane was also there. The father and son looked nothing like each other. The old man was tall, black, and losing his dreads. He had no hair down the center of his head, just long, scraggly braids down both sides covering his ears. Roots was a big fair skinned Rastas man with a face as speckled as an overripe banana. Both of them were useless. They did no work. They just walked around and got in the way of the people and the children who were doing most of the cleaning. I saw the whole thing as a delightful experiment, a warm-up for that aptitude test next week.

Just before I started to put on the paints, Elder Kallai Cush interrupted me to recited this verse as a benediction to the work:

> Behold! Jah is our mirror
> Open your eyes and see them in him
> And learn the manner of your face in
> Him
> And tell forth praise to His spirit
> And wipe off Babylon from your faces
> And love His holiness, and clothe
> yourselves
> Therewith and be without the stain
> of Babylon
> At all times before Him. Jah...

Everything I wanted on the walls was already there, sketched in fine lines. It took me that whole week to finish the application of the paints. In places where I needed motion, I would brush back against the bumps on the walls and allow the strokes to flow up. The finished work sat there covered up with old bed sheets, protected from flying dust. We unveiled the arrangement that Saturday evening, just before the congregation showed up for the regular service.

Elder Kallai Cush entered the church dressed in a long flowing African robe. He walked to the pulpit with Roots Mane at his side. He stood, and raised his hands for silence. "We took an important step this week, and Jah blessed us. Some of you already know Whitfield. You have been working with him all week. It's hard to call him anything but a brother. He made a joyous contribution to this chapel. Whitfield, come up here. Let everyone look at you with their eyes and see Jah in you. I & I."

I went forward and stood between Kallai Cush and his son, Roots Mane. I felt awkward looking at the many faces staring up. Some black as night, others brown as rich chocolate, and some as yellow as gold. All dressed in clean clothes with their children at their sides. I felt moist in the pit of my arms. I wondered how long I would have to stand before them, and what they might be thinking about me, this Johnny-Come-lately.

"This is a proper day for a Grounation!" Elder Kallai Cush said. "April twenty-first. Jah Ras Tafari came out of the east with the rising sun on this day. He visited the lost tribe in Jamaica. We ask for a consecration on this ground and on all those present here today, Jah."

The assembled, more than seventy-five of them, they sat quietly for a long time looking at the images on the walls. The applause that rose out of the silence forced me to breathe deep. Flyn was looking at me with a half smile on his face, and Melba was clapping as if trying to turn her hands red. I had no idea that there could be such joy in a bunch of people hitting their hands together. As I looked at the room and the many faces, I saw my power apparent for the first time.

The mural and the people brought the room alive. Hope and pride filled the place and I was a part of that. The paints covered three quarters of the room--in black, gold, green, red and blue. It came together on the walls of the rectangular room swarming its lines, a tide of swirling colors.

On one wall, a slave galleon rode angry blue waves. Black bodies suspended in the space above the plunging blue of the ocean, as if thrown from the ship. On the other wall, what looked like cane stretched to its full extent, and approaching the canes were black stick figures with hands holding machetes high. Little white figures stood by with whips and guns. The rendition was simple, but the message was powerful.

The final touches on the composition sat behind the pulpit. Two large portraits, one of Haile Selassie, bearded dreadlocks, the other of Marcus Garvey, dressed in a dashiki; hair dreaded in long manes. Their arms extended as if embracing both sides of the assembly.

The service started in honest with a circle of prayer. Everyone moved out to the walls, holding hands. This gave me a chance to escape the scrutiny. I moved away from the old man and his son, to a point near Flyn and Melba and fitted myself into the circle. Roots Mane led the prayer; it lasted for almost five minutes. The circle broke as Elder Kallai shouted: "Jah! Ras-Ta-fari." And started singing with a big bass voice. The congregation joined him in song:

> Ethiopia thou land of our father
> Thou land where the Gods love to be
> As storm clouds at night sudden
> Our armies come rushing to thee.
> With the red/gold/and green floating o'er us
> And the emperor to shield us from wrong
> With a God and a future before us.
> We hail and we shout with this song.

The congregation coupled with this refrain. They moved back to their seats with voices swelled:

> Long lives our Negus, Negus I.
> And keep Ethiopia free to advance

> To advance with truth and right,
> To advance with truth and light,
> With righteous leading we hasten to our
> God and king humanity pleading one God
> For us all.

The singing came to an abrupt end, and Elder Kallai Cush moved into position to begin his sermon. I just couldn't wait to hear what the old man had to say. My impression of liberation always meant a fight of some sort. Masters will always fight to keep their slaves. Pharaoh fought to keep his property. God wants us to fight that battle? Will He part the Atlantic; allow us to march back to Africa? I wanted to hear the words of the old man.

"This place where we meet to seek the highest is holy ground," the old man began. "We are here today to celebrate an occasion that's both blessed and determining. This is the anniversary of the ascension of Ras Tafari. They tried to tell us that he's dead, but how can men kill God? We saw no body. They held no funeral. He just left this earth and took his rightful place in heaven. I&I. Jah, Ras Tafari. What we Rastas must reconcile is the meeting of history and faith. I for one choose faith. I remember Jah in the earth, in the rain and in the sun, the absolute child of mother Africa. Kings of kings, elect of God, Defender of our Faith.

"We the children of mother Africa came from a race who walked the same ground where these Scriptures were born. Our ancestors took the Ark of the Covenant back to their homeland; build churches and cities of stone. Prayed to the one God, Jah, and repulsed invaders that came to shed their blood. We learned from the Kebra Negast that a queen from Ethiopia visited Solomon and came back bearing his child, making all this possible, and paving the way for Ras Tarfari, making it necessary for us to be here today. History and faith my brethren, history and faith. This is the place where they meet.

"In the first book of Kings, chapter one, verse ten, they tell us of the communion between Solomon and Sheba. Have no doubts that we are Christians, and worshipers of the one God called Jah. In the New Testament, chapter eight of the Acts of the Apostles they tell us of the first Ethiopian Christian baptized by the apostle Philip. From the Scriptures according to Jeremiah, chapter eight, verse twenty-one, we know that Jah is everything and black. 'For the hurt of the daughters of my people am I hurt; I am black; astonishment hath taken hold of me . . . ' they further state it in Daniel, chapter seven, verse nine. They tell us of the last king of kings: 'And I beheld till the throne was cast down where the Ancient of Days did sit, whose garment was white as snow, and the hair of his head like pure lamb's wool . . . ' Come out, come out of Babylon you sons and daughters of Africa. He speaks of you. You heard it in the words of Jah. Jah has chosen you to inherit this world. It's as plain as day in Psalms Eighty-seven. 'His foundation is in these holy mountains. Glorious things are spoken of thee, O city of God Selah. I will make mention of Rehab and Babylon to them that know me: Behold Philistia, and Tyre, with Ethiopia; this man was born there . . . this man on whom He has already bestowed his greatest gifts... Jah loves. This world is yours. All you have to do is find the courage to reach out and take it."

Elder Kallai Cush snatched at the crowd with his fingers set as claw, then he pulled his fist into his chest and stepped back from the pulpit. I was disappointed. He spoke of liberation in such oblique terms. The service melted into music, drums, tambourines and maracas. They accompanied voices that reminded me of a Shango or a revival meeting back home. The singing lasted for more than thirty minutes, smiling, relaxed, some swayed to the music, others danced openly. Now and then, a voice in the crowd would shout: "I&I. Jah, Ras Tafari!"

The service seemed to be everlasting. The testimonies about the work of Jah in their lives were touching. Two small boys made the rounds with a tray; the parishioners dug in their pockets and filled the containers with money. Relief washed over me as the service left the ritual phase and ebbed into what Flyn called fellowship.

We shared a vegetarian supper. Elder Kallai Cush blessed the food. After the meal, the old man led Flyn, Roots Mane, and me to a side room. Flyn raised his shirt and unbuckled a belt with many pockets. He took out the biggest wad of money I've ever seen. He placed the bills in neat piles on the table, then they counted the cash in the trays. Elder Kallai took some of the money, and handed it to me for the work on the mural. I refused. The old man smiled.

"Jah sent you here, Whitfield. Remember these words." He pointed his finger at Roots and Flyn. "I see Jah at work here." The old man spoke as he handed the money back to Flyn. "Take good care of this, brother, and don't be tempted," he smiled. "In a few days we will call a Nyabingi, assemble the congregation to decide who goes to Sha Shamane. Drop me home, son." The old man turned his back to leave.

"I don't see why we doing this. That I'll only cause hard feelings," Roots said. "One day we'll need this money real bad. You pilgrimage to Sha Shamane, dad. Let Flyn come if he wants too. We can't spend..."

"You short sighted, son," the old man interrupted Roots. "Just leave this to me."

"But dad--"

"Leave this to me, Roots."

Roots face fell down into a mask of resignation. He looked back at Flyn and me briefly as if he wanted to say more, but he followed his father.

"What was that?"

"Must be the father and son war? Like king David and his other son, not Solomon, the other one, Absalom. Roots have other ideas for this church. His father doesn't trust him because of his former drug problems. I don't trust him for another reason. He acts stupid at times, acts without thinking things through."

"That's a lot of money," I said to Flyn. I changed the subject because all of his Biblical comments sailed right over my head, and his remarks about Roots made me uneasy. "Why don't you put that money in a bank?"

"We don't believe in banks," he said. "I'll keep this safe, right here. All ten thousand. If the house is ever on fire, I keep the money in the wall behind the bedroom closet. Grab it if am not there," he smiled.

"All that cash makes me nervous," I said.

Flyn shrugged his shoulders, placed the wad of bills back in the belt, and tucked it under his shirt.

"Don't worry about it, man."

We headed for the door. Flyn took me down town and familiarized me with the bus routes. That's how I would be getting to school and back, and to work when I found a job.

I could hardly wait for Monday. I had no idea what an aptitude test looked like, but I knew it would be nothing. After finishing that mural, I felt like a million dollars. I could do anything. Flyn dropped me off at the school on his way to work that Monday.

The test was nothing. However, it took forever before they gave it to me, then they looked at my old stuff and stared talking as if I wasn't in the same room with them. They started to chatter about Haitian and African art, using the word primitive. These people who gave me the test looked nothing like artists. They wore suits and ties, clothes I was sure they didn't want to get paint on. They asked me how many more drawing I had at home. I said just a few, but I had dozens. They told me to frame them; they knew a gallery that would take some of them, sell them to help pay for my schooling. By the time I left the place late that afternoon, I was seeing dollars, lots of Yankee dollars, big piles of greenbacks, bigger than the piles in Flyn's belt. All that money was on my brain. I left the school and took the wrong bus. So, I had to go back downtown and wait for the right one. It was almost five o'clock before I got back to Flyn and Melba's.

I came around the corner and I slowed when I noticed the crowd in front of the house. The wooden fence was broken down and strewn. About twelve Rastafarians with machetes, sticks and stones stood on the sidewalk staring at the house. A few neighbors stood across the street, looking on. I rushed into the crowd. Roots Mane with his big rusty looking head of dreads stood in the yard near the house. The place looked wrecked, and mangled. All the front windows were broken. I spoke to the Rastas man nearest me as I came into the yard.

"What happened? Where's Flyn, where's Melba?"

The man looked at me hard, big rocks in both hands. He said nothing. I turned to head straight for the front door. The Rastafrians closed ranks, and steered me down with stone faces. Roots Mane moved back from the house and came up behind the Rastas who were blocking my path. He looked at me, and recognition slid down his face.

"That bombocloth no want to give we the money, Whitfield," Roots pointed at the house. "He talking 'bout somebody stole it. I don't believe him. That's your uncle. Talk to him."

"What the hell, Roots? That's Flyn. Is he in the house? Where's Melba? Did somebody call the police?"

Roots looked at me again, and frowned. "Babylon na have nothing to do with we business. Both in there. Go in, talk some sense into them. Tell them to come out. We want we money now."

I looked at the circle of angry Rastas, then at the house. I found it hard to believe that the very people who prayed and sang songs just two days ago had done such damage. The glass from the broken windows was everywhere on the grass. I found Flyn and Melba barricaded in the bedroom. They crawled out slowly when they heard my voice. Inside, the house was completely ransacked. Flyn bled from a cut on his left arm. Melba wrapped a towel around it.

"Flyn, those guys out there–"

"We came home and found the place like this. Somebody stole the money, all of it. You didn't see it, did you, Whitfield?"

I shook my head.

"I had it back there where I told you," Flyn pointed at the closet. "I'm a dead man. I'm a dead man for sure." He turned and slumped on the edge of the bed. Melba hugged his shoulder.

"We have to think, Flyn. We have to think," she kept repeating.

"Those fellows out there," I said. "They have cutlass and big stones. Elder Kallai could make them behave. You have his number? Where's the telephone?"

"He sent them, Whitfield. We called him right after we noticed the money was gone. Ten minutes later the first stone came through the window," Melba said.

"Where's the phone? I have to try talking to him."

Melba found the phone under a pile of books. She dialed a number and handed the receiver to me. The voice on the other end of the wire answered flat and at ease.

"Elder Kallai? This is Whitfield Malotte."

"What can I do for you, Whitfield?"

"Elder, a group of Rastas outside Flyn's and Melba's house causing trouble. They stoned the place, broke all the windows. Flyn is hurt. Bleeding." I was listening to the man breathing on the other end of the wire, and I had a bad feeling. He was taking too long to speak.

"This is out of my hands, Whitfield. It's in the hands of Jah now."

"What you mean, Elder? Didn't you hear me? They want to kill Flyn."

Another long pause. I guess I didn't quite believe Melba at first.

"Did you send them, Elder?" The phone remained silent. "You want the money back? I don't see how killing Flyn can get you that. I'll have the money for you tomorrow," I heard myself saying.

Another lingering silence, then Elder Kallai spoke. "Whitfield, I expect to see you tomorrow, before noon, in the temple. Have the money in cash. If not you will be a marked man, along with your uncle and his woman. You understand me?"

"I understand you. Now call off your gang, please." I heard the phone click in my ears. I shook my head at the sound of the conch shell. Just a bit more of the Islands. The Rastas started walking away from the house.

"We have to get you to a doctor, Flyn. That cut looks really bad," I said.

"To hell with the doctor," he said. His eyes were ablaze. He looked as though he might leap off the bed at me. It was the first time I had seen my uncle upset. "You told him you will bring him the money tomorrow. Where's the money?"

"I don't know, Flyn."

"Well what did you do with it?"

"I never had it."

"What the hell you trying to do? Give me the money now."

Melba was looking at me hard as if she would help Flyn beat the money out of me, but then she spoke.

"Flyn, wait. Look at Whitfield. He's only trying to help," she said.

"Jesus Christ Whitfield! You shouldn't have done that. This isn't your business." His eyes softened. "This isn't happening? Where are we going to find--?"

"I would have said anything to make them go away," I said. "Let's get you to the hospital before you bleed to death. We can figure out the money later."

We came out of the house and started across the yard to the car. As we approached the smashed fence, Roots Mane emerged from the shelter of the hedge near the house. He surprised mc. I looked at the man as he positioned himself between the car and us, a machete one hand.

"Where you going so fast? Sneaking out to spend the money already?"

He stood there glaring at me, Flyn and Melba. The blade at his side. He moved toward us across the yard. Flyn and I backed up as Roots advanced with the blade raised. Melba held her ground for a moment, and then she moved left to let him pass. She was looking around, frantic. Her lips were moving wordlessly. She grabbed a piece of the downed fence and charged at Roots Mane from behind. She swung the post with all her might into his ribs and back. She stumbled on impact;

fell backwards onto her hunches. Roots just flinched slightly and turned on Melba with the machete.

He didn't have to raise his arm. The machete was already in the air. It happened in one blinding instant. He started to lower the blade on Melba as she scrambled away. Flyn screamed and rushed toward Melba. I snatched a piece of the splintered wood and threw it like a spear. It connected with the side of Roots' face. The arch of the blade sliced near Melba as she regained her footing and stumbled into Flyn. Roots fell to his knees with one hand clutching his face. Blood oozed through his fingers. I grabbed another piece of the fence because he still held the machete in his other hand. Melba snatched another piece of the fence and came at Roots again. Our blows connected with him simultaneously. The machete fell out of his hand and his shirt flew open. A pile of money tumbled out of a belt strapped around his waist, and settled at his feet. The group of Rastas that had charged back to help Roots stood dumbfounded.

"Your money," Flyn pointed at the ground. "You want to chop me up. Roots stole the money. Look at him," Flyn shouted hysterically, kicking at the strewn bills. "You sons of bitches, take him, get him out my yard. Bunch of hypocrites. Thanks you very much. Thank you, brothers." Flyn spat the words at them.

Melba and I stood with the pieces of the fence clutched in our hands. One man dragged Roots to his feet, the others collected the money, and they walked away with a hand gripping the back of Roots neck. Not one of them glanced back at Flyn as they moved off. Melba started to cry. She looked at the piece of wood in her hand, then she threw it to the ground as if discarding a snake. Flyn placed his good arm around her.

It took twelve stitches to close the cut on Flyn's arm. We went down to Melba's grandmother's restaurant after leaving the hospital. It seemed the news had already made the rounds of the neighborhood. A stout old woman in an apron greeted us, placed us at a corner table and brought food. She shook her head constantly as she served the food. Not asking any questions.

"I hope you two learned something from this. You have no right hanging around with that bunch. You have good educations and the whole future ahead of you. Don't let this damage your faith in God though. He works in mysterious ways. His wonders to perform. Well you both still alive. I hope this taught you a lesson. Who is this?"

The old woman spoke as she stood near the table looking down at us. Flyn with his bandaged arm in a sling, Melba with a kerchief dabbing her face, and me wondering how all this could've happened. The old woman stared me down as the question left her mouth.

"This is Flyn's nephew, Nana. We told you about him." Melba answered, her nose sniffling. Now that the whole thing was over Melba appeared so delicate and vulnerable. But in the heat of the fight . . . I felt so proud of her. I just wanted to throw my arms around her.

"Oh yeah, the Grenadian?" the old woman said, and extended a hard looking bony hand. I stood and took her hand.

"Mam," I said. I disengaged my hand from her firm grip and sat.

Flyn and Melba threw embarrassed glances at the old woman. She didn't seem to care. She continued to talk to them in admonishing tones.

"Where will you all stay tonight? I send a couple fellows up there to put some plywood on the windows. Keep the rain out."

"We'll stay at the house. We need to clean up a little," Melba said.

The old woman looked at us again. "You be careful. You hear me? I have customers." She spoke as she walked away through swinging doors and into the back. She came back, stuck her head over the doors. "Melba, you on this shift tomorrow."

"I know, Nana. See you then."

We ate the food slowly, lingering. Curried goat with rice and red beans. Washed it down with ginger beer. From the restaurant, we went straight back to the house. The men that Nana had dispatched were already gone. The place looked blind and woeful. Melba gathered a few things, swept some glass off the floor.

No one reached for the radio or television. Melba said nothing as she swept the floor. I found it strange. Neither Flyn nor Melba mentioned Roots Mane or the money. I recalled the voice of Kallia Cush on the phone. It's in the hands of Jah. I thought it would be quite all right if I never saw the man again. I contemplated how good it would feel to seek in and paint over the mural. Nevertheless, on second thought, I concluded that leaving it alone would be better. Let the prophets gaze down on them; reproach them with those eyes.

I took a beer out of the refrigerator and sat at the kitchen table. I shook my head, and exhaled hard as if to expel the day's troubles. Flyn came walking into the kitchen. I looked at him lugging his damaged arm as if it were some kind of trophy. He had a pleasant look on his face. I felt compelled to ask him a question, but before the words could leave my mouth, Flyn spoke, and pointed at the beer in my hand.

"I need one of them tonight. Will you open it for me? Melba went to sleep. She's exhausted from all the excitement."

I reached into the fridge. Flyn sat across the table from me. He looked as if he would smile at any moment. Excitement, he called it. I looked at the place in shambles, and I felt as violated as if this was my house.

"What you going to do now?" I asked. "About the Ethiopians Assembly and your trip to Sha Shamane?"

He still carried that look of ease on his face.

"Nothing," he said. "I'm a Rasta man in good standing. My conscience is clear. We'll make the trip some day. But not with them."

"You just going to take all that?"

"In my life there's no room to carry grudges, Whitfield."

"You amaze me, Flyn. I was thinking we might go over there and burn the place down. What you say?"

He smiled at me.

"The first thing I tell people when I mediate any dispute. Learn to forgive. Break the chain."

"I was just joking about burning the place down."

"I know."

"I've this feeling sometimes. It's like my presence caused things to happen? Bad things. My being in this world has caused a lot of grief. I know that."

"Oh really! I see where you going with that." He had a droll tone in his voice. "You are no more responsible for the actions of Roots Mane, Kallia Cush and a few stray Rastas than you are for the actions of Vince Malotte and my father. Lay your burden down, Whitfield." His expression reminded me of someone on the brink of laugher but thought better of it. "My mother charged me with the task of saying something to you when I thought the time was right," he said. "She thought you might digest it easier, coming from me instead of from one of your aunts. She thought you had the right to know."

He was leaning forward in the chair, still looking at me. He folded the fingers on his good hand around the bottle of beer as if to take a swig, but he just kept it there.

"I know you know most of it, so I will just touch on the things I'm sure you don't realize. Vince and Nails were good friends. Nails admired Vince. He wanted this smart young man to marry one of his daughters. Nails wanted to handpick the men who would marry his daughters, but Vince went for the wrong one. Nails had no idea that his young friend would go after his daughter who was almost a Child. My mother found out and tried to take Jean to the Voodoo woman up in Jan Anglais. You know, to get a portion to throw away the child . . ." He paused.

I was listening to him speak. He sounded as if referring to another person instead of me. He started talking again, but now he kept his eyes on a spot behind my back on the wall.

"Jean refused to do what our mother said, and Nails overheard them quarreling. He forced Jean to tell him who the man was. He invited Vince to go hunting, and no one saw him after that day. Rumors started flying about Jean's big belly and how Vince was the only man to get close enough to her. Everyone said Vince must have stowaway on a vessel headed to Trinidad, and is now hiding from Nails in Port of Spain or San Fernando.

They found Vince some months later. A big rainstorm full of thunder and lightening washed the body out of the ground where Nails had buried it. He buried Vince standing up straight, in a narrow hole. So many stories went around. Your grandmother had to listen to all of them. She lost her husband and her daughter as a result. She got you to replace them. Can you imagine how she felt, looking at you? Thinking about all that came to pass?"

"Yeah, I can more than imagine. I remember how she looked at me. Those eyes. What a thing. There must be something special for me to do in this world? That's the reason I'm here."

"Probably," he smiled. "But that doesn't mean you should remain shackled to all that."

He finally looked at me again, and then he raised the beer to his lips as if in some kind of salute. He brought the bottle back down to the table quietly. In that instant, I grasp why my uncle held no animosity toward me for the death of his father. So strange, the guilt I carried, but things are becoming more apparent.

I'm learning how to breathe more comfortably. Amen to all that. Tomorrow is another day.

TOETAGS

Dear Oscar:

I never imagined anything like this. I assumed a fine. I need your help to get out of here. I'll be eternally grateful if you would respond to this letter. My conduct toward you in the courtroom was unforgivable. Things like apologies and asking for help don't come easy for me.

The first few days here was really a bitch. A couple of words from an old country song got stuck in my head. Hello walls. Hello walls. I couldn't remember the other words or who sung the song. Hello walls. Hello walls.

The paint bubbled and ran, forming a huge face. The judge's, the psychiatrist's and yours, mixed up as one. That was the night they fed me a little blue pill. It took me awhile to come to my senses. You had nothing to do with what happened to me. Okay?

They took the drugs away two days ago. The doctor is trying another form of therapy. He wants me to write. I'll show the bastard. He played right into my hands.

Officialdom! What a crock? Old fools making decisions for me. Treating me like a child. I should have known. I've been there before. *You'll stay confined until a doctor verifies that you are no longer a threat to society'.* The old judge sat up there on his high bench, in his black robe. Vicious owl. I felt like smashing his face. They took me away as he ordered.

Then, that doctor started: Purge, banish that anger, seek the truth'. He looked puffy, like a sponge cake, could be gay. This had to be his first job out of college. I'm sure he had pimples on his ass. What could he tell me about anything?

I wanted to shout at him, 'boy, truth is highly over rated. Truth is a rip-off. There's always a price and that price is exactly the passion you can't afford to relinquish. Anger is my clothing. You can't ask a man to go naked'.

The young doctor asked me, how do you see your life, in the past, in the future'. He had me stumped. What the fuck kind of question is that? Another silly little melody sat at the front of my mind: This little light of mine . . . it blocked everything, caused a wicked hum inside my head. 'Straight, paved roads', I said to him. Blooming flowers. I've always liked those'. The words came out of my mouth at the young doctor like fists shadowboxing, and instantly silence came into my head.

'This should be a cinch then', he said through a wet little laugh. 'You'll have to kneel down,' figuratively I mean, 'as if in prayer. Cull the lies. Resolve that conversation with the little man inside your head. Find out what's the truth for you'. And he reached into a draw on the side of his desk.

Man alive. He handed me this yellow legal pad, and this pencil? Imagine giving a madman like me a sharp pencil? Translate thirty-two years of anger and the effort it took to disguise it. He laid that task before me. I'll give him what he wants, Lord knows he deserves it. But I can't just surrender to this confrontation.

Oscar, people like him have always pissed me off. They immerse themselves in their neat little lives like flies on shit, hardly aware that it would take so little to fuck it all up. A wrong turn, a harsh word, staring just too long at the wrong person.

Most people don't have the slightest idea how dangerous this life can be. If they only realize, they would hide under their beds with their children huddled close, never coming out, not even to take a crap.

Oh, you must be thinking, where does courage fit into all this? Courage is pure bullshit. I've seen brave people die just as easy as cowards. It's all the same in the end. Dead is dead. Only the imagination of the living feeds that dog called heroism. I was a mortician you see. That profession has conferred on me a decisive attitude toward the living and the dead. We are more human in death than we are in life.

My one inheritance from my family came from my uncle Sydney. He bestowed it on me in four simple words. 'Learn to type, boy', he had said. 'Uncle Sam will come calling. If you know how to type no one will ever shoot at you'.

I took his advice, and enrolled in typing classes in high school. Took some serious ribbing for that, but more important, I met some sensational girls. When Uncle Sam did come calling, I ended up in a morgue in the Philippines processing dead people. Three years in that refrigerated warehouse of formaldehyde and talcum. It seems like a lifetime now. Through it all, my friend Ben Lane was there. He is dead now, God rests his soul, and I'm in this place. I regret not being able to attend his funeral. Pardon the cliché, but life is certainly a bitch sometimes.

So, Oscar, look this over. I hope we are protected by attorney client privilege. I'm not trying to drag you into a conspiracy or anything, but you understand judges and doctors better than I do. And the sooner I'm out of here, the sooner I can get the rest of your money to you. I don't know what the hell to tell them. This all began for me the day my mother pointed a shotgun at my father and pulled the trigger.

* * *

That was my twelfth birthday gift. I went catatonic in the face of death. But miraculously, I didn't die. I woke up a few days later, wandering in a deep dark place, dragging some heavy memories, memories of a potent fear that forced me to shit in my pants. I remember it well. I swore never to do that again, and I developed a strategy. I could stay safe and strong under these conditions. I told myself: Keep those jaws clinched. Let determination etch furrows on your forehead. Eyes must remain vicious slits, and there must be the absolute conviction set in these bones that if anyone fucked with me I could kill them. It was that simple.

Once you have known violent death, it's no longer a stranger. Death became the sole member of my family.

I once thought of my family as ordinary. There were my mother, my father, and my little brother, Harry. The only other person in our family who came around from time to time was Uncle Sydney, my mother's brother. All the other members of her family disowned her after she married my father, Robert Grant, a black man. There was one aspect to interracial marriage that my mother never recognized. If you marry a black man and have children, you have effectively switched races. Your loyalty is to the race that will sustain you progeny, not to the one that will seek to oppress them.

My father was always out of work. And this time he hadn't worked in six months. He called things like dishwashing and lawn mowing, kids jobs. He equated that kind of labor with working in the fast-food industry. No real man should ever have to do that kind of work, he'd say. He was waiting for that job at the pulp-mill, at the university or at the mental hospital. Waiting for Publisher's clearinghouse or Reader's Digest to pay him all of those millions.

My mother thought he was kind of foolish and she never hesitated to tell him. That's when he would start slapping her around. Her eyes would swell and turn black and blue. Her lips would puff up and bleed. But then the swelling would go away. Her natural color would return and everything would be just fine, until the next fight. They fought endlessly, viciously, over nothing, and neither ever won. They looked like boxers with all the cuts and bruises. My father would be on the couch sulking when we left for school in the morning and he'd be there when we returned around four in the evening.

We had to fight him just to watch cartoons. We usually lost. I still hate Television.

They say my mother shot him on that couch. I've always wondered about the dealings that transpired that day. Could it have been an attempt on her part, to return to who she was before marrying my father? If she divorced him, she would still be left with us as symbols of her transgressions.

We came home from school early that day. My little brother Harry always led the way after the bus dropped us off. He sure could run. He'd race up the road, feet pelting, that bag of books bouncing on his back. I always wondered what drew him to that house, so fast, each evening. After all this time, I still carry this guilt. He's dead and I'm alive because he loved to run.

I heard the first shot as we approached the house. Harry was way ahead of me. He looked back, and then he rushed up the stairs to the front door. I heard him shout, "mom! Then he came flying backwards through the screen door as if kicked in the stomach by a horse. Books flew everywhere. A big red splotch seeped out across the front of his shirt. He was on the ground at the bottom of the stairs, on his back.

I don't recall hearing the report of the shotgun a second time. But Harry was on the ground bleeding. I ran to him and knelt down placing my hand on his chest to stop the blood. His eyes were wide open. He looked surprised. He kept trying to catch his breath. Blood bubbled out of his mouth and nose with each pant. I heard the steps and I looked back over my shoulder. She stood on the stairs with the gun in her hand. Her pink terry cloth robe opened down the front. Her old checkered apron skewed to one side.

The face I saw was not my mother's. There was something like a foul grin. Tears ran down her cheeks mixing with spittle at the corners of lips folded back against teeth. She looked as if she might growl. I needed her to speak. If she spoke, I knew everything would be all right. When she didn't speak, I whispered. "Mom?"

When I die, that face will be the last thing I see, and I hate that. Her eyes were on fire and the tears must have boiled, burning deep gullies down her cheeks as they ran. This was not a face. The skin was like plastic pulled tight across fierce bones. I was still down on my knees next to Harry. He shuddered under my hands and I looked away from my mother. Harry's blood covered my fingers. I swallowed and my stomach heaved, my mouth filled, overflowing my lips. My hand reached up to block the flow of vomit. The warm juice seeped through my fingers, and down my chin onto the front of my shirt.

She raised the gun, and the dirt next to me jumped. Then I heard, click, click. Her lips moved but no words came out. My knees were frozen to the ground. I was torn between leaving Harry and running for my life. When she started digging in her apron pocket to reload the gun, a sudden urge pulled me upright, and I darted around the corner of the house.

She didn't even glance at Harry. She came after me, hands out of her pocket, reloading the gun as she walked. I dove under the house. The dirt was dry, hard packed beneath my fingers and knees. I crawled into a far corner. The muzzle-flash forced me to close my eyes.

I folded my arms across my ears and nose too late. To this day, the stink of sulfur still makes me nauseous. I'm dead, I thought. So, I rolled into a ball, hid my face, and sunk into darkness.

I woke up to the sound of a stranger's voice calling my name. I was no longer under the house. I was sure of that. I must be coming back from a long strange dream? A woman with powder on her face told me everything would be fine. For weeks, she kept pounding me with questions, forcing me to talk. Finally, she asked me if I wanted to see my mother. The sound of the gun, the small flashes, the stink, all still with me. Images, painful and refined. My mother stood on the stairs with a gun, Harry under my hand with a red hole in his body. The fear in my chest as heavy as a stone. I said very little, but she kept talking to me, day after day. She took me on a trip and showed me two graves.

It took me a long time to agree to see my mother. And it was only after I had reconstructed everything in my head. Those details came back to me like small electric charges that would jolts me. It was like sitting quietly and suddenly experiencing a series of little convulsions. My body actually flinched at those moments.

I don't know why I agreed to see her. It must have been to feed those angry beasts growling inside my gut. Shamed and anger choked me. I knew then that I would live as I dream. Alone.

When I saw her, she appeared normal. She looked like my mother again, in ordinary clothes, sitting there with a cigarette between her lips. The skin on her face relaxed. I had no idea what to say to her. They left us in a small room together. The silence stood between us like a snarling dog. She spoke first, through teeth stained brown. Her eyes hooded by smoke from the cigarette.

"How they treating you, son?"

"Okay."

"They say we might be going home soon." She said the words not looking at me. There was the hint of a smile on one side of her face. I had the impression that her words meant more than the obvious.

They released us from the hospital and we were back living together. A social worker came by from time to time. One day my mother said to me, 'I had hopes once. I didn't realize it was something you could spend, like money. And it can run out'. She was standing in the kitchen with her back to me, mixing mayonnaise and tuna fish, scooping it onto plain white bread. My mother hated whole wheat. The sandwich tasted funny to me but I ate it anyway. The rat poison she had folded into the food didn't kill me. She had an ulcer and started bleeding internally. I know now that that is not a pleasant way to die. My uncle Sydney became my legal guardian.

Sydney took me in because I had an income. The man acted like prey. He moved about with a scurrying gait, eyes darting here and there. His pattern of speech matched his deportment. He spoke in staccato burst, punctuated by gaps of silence. It had the effect of stuttering but not quite. He looked nothing like my mother. Sydney claimed to be a professional gambler. Not a good one I presumed because he owed everyone. My junior year in high school, he left town for Los Vegas, to attend an event known as the World Series of Poker. A maid found him hanging from his hotel balcony. He had cut several towels into strips, which he braided into a stout rope.

No one attended my graduation. I'm the last of my family, or at least that branch of it. With the help of a teacher called Mister Brigs, I enrolled in college, but the whole thing was just too mundane and sedentary. I did horribly. Uncle Sam decided a man of my stature should not go to waste. So, I got one of those cute greetings. Drafted into the man's Army. That's where I met Ben Lane, the man partially responsible for me being in this fix.

Our friendship had a strange beginning. It started in a bar on Luzon. Some Jarhead kept mouthing off at us. The man had no respect for the dead. And he was so fucking annoying with that nasal voice. He sounded like a dull saw going through wood. He kept talking shit about touching dead people. He got really morbid, started making jokes about having a cold one, just about accused us of fucking the corpses. I lost my temper and smashed my beer on his face. Hitting him was a bad idea. There were two of us, and a bunch of them. The M.Ps. dragged us out of there barely alive. I felt exhilarated, purged. Ben and I became steadfast friends after that. I got us into many more fight just for the hell of it.

We received our discharge papers one month apart. He invited me to come to Montana, help him run his family funeral home. There was nothing left in Oklahoma for me. And Norman would have been the last place in the world I would have returned to. I made it out there just in time for his wedding to Chareth Smith. The poor bastard.

In the end, she took the children and most of his money. I ended up with the funeral home after the cops busted Ben with a pound of pot. His license was revoked. He thought it would be a good idea if I bought him out, said he needed the money to move to Missoula. Make a new start, in a bigger place.

I'm no expert on women, but Ben never understood the first thing about females. He thought they were just like men. I've tried for years to acquaint him with the other side of women. The man never learned.

Best friends, close buddies. He died without knowing that he was more intimate with me than with his own wife, and I'm not gay. Our beer drinking sprees, hunting and fishing trips, Our idle road trips to Kalispell and Missoula just to sit in bars, getting high, doing shots, all this added up to more than he gave to his wife. We never took her on any of our excursions. And after the children were born . . . Poor Chareth. When she left, I asked her why Bakersfield, she said she liked the name.

I can't help thinking that maybe if Ben and I had never met he might still be alive. He would have returned from the service, run the funeral home and married Chareth. But there I was, like some kind of spoiler. When she left with the children, the man fell apart. He started drinking more. We always drank draft beers, but he started drinking Gran Marnier, Drambuie and imported beers. He got careless with pot.

I knew Ben was in trouble long before he did. At the funeral home, Chareth did makeup. I did the embalming, the dressing and some cremations. Ben was the front man. He spoke to people, made sure all the details were handled, attended memorial services etc. One day when he was out at a grave sight, Chareth and I sat down for a cup of coffee. From out of nowhere she slapped me with the strangest question.

"Jere, do you ever think of breathing?"

"What?"

"Breathing, you know taking air and letting it out."

"I know what breathing is. I don't think about it. It's automatic."

"My point exactly," she said. "Breathing is one of the fundamentals of human life but we ignore it. You know it could be the cure for all kinds of ills. Ulcers, cancers, the common cold. I believe books can be written on the subject. For all we know there could be a hidden disease known as shallow breathing. The sufferers live shorter lives, contract more ailments . . . "

Can a woman with a mind that works like that stay married to a man who constantly ignored her? He paid more attention to corpses. Why didn't I say something? How could I? I was part of their problem. I know that now. I'm confounded that Chareth never said a word to me or showed any resentment. If she ever spoke to Ben about my presence in their life, he never mentioned it.

It took Ben about one year to drink himself to death. The cops found him sitting in an alley in Missoula. He was bruised and bleeding, crusted blood down his left temple, legs curled up in front of him. In late winters that is not the place to fall asleep. The report concluded with one word. Hypothermia.

His mother asked me to retrieve the body, and I almost refused. The drive to Missoula and back should have taken about three hours. Routine kind of thing. Pickup the body, drive back to Mark Tree. But no. It couldn't be that simple. Not for me. He was my friend. He got me started in the business. If I only knew, I would have stuffed his dead ass in the hearse and drove away. But no. I wanted to have a last celebration with my friend. That's when my problems began.

This would be our last road trip, so I didn't think it strange to park the hearse outside the bar, have a couple beers before taking him home. Lukes was our favorite bar when we came to town. I thought of taking him in and propping him up in a chair, but I didn't think the patrons would understand.

The bartender was a skinny woman with a face like a horse. I had never seen her before. She stood behind the bar talking to a big red-faced fellow. I ordered a draft and a shot of Jack. She ignored me and red-face looked at me as if I was some kind of fool for disturbing their conversation.

"I'll be back," he said to her, still glaring at me as he walked toward the door. Either a chronic drunk or a severe case of Rosaceae, I thought.

By the time I was finished with the second draft, no shot that time, a voice from behind my back asked: "Whose hearse is that out there?" I turned to see two cops making their way across the half empty bar. I stood, faced them and in my sturdiest voice answered, "That's my hearse."

"Sir, we have a report that there's a body in the hearse. Is it alive or dead?"

"What the hell would a live man be doing laid out in a hearse?"

"Don't give us any lip, sir. Remove the hearse, take the body back to the morgue if you going to be drinking. You are causing a public disturbance. Look out there. You see that crowd?"

I'll be damned if a crowd hadn't gathered. And everyone in the bar followed me out. They stood looking into the hearse. All they could see was his feet. They stuck out from under the cover, pale white, and bluish. The cops got into their car as I moved around to the driver's side of the hearse. The crowd stood in my path.

"What the fuck you people looking at. Get the fuck away from there. Move, move; you bunch of fucking clowns."

They seemed shocked: old ladies, middle-aged men and women on lunch break, on their way to blow a few bucks on video keno or poker. I pushed my way into the little crowd toward the driver's door. They moved back like vultures pulling away from a carcass.

"Who the hell you think you are? Talking to us like that."

The question came from that same big, red-face fellow. He was standing there looking at me, his back to the side window of the hearse. I ignored the question but the guy wouldn't leave it alone. He stepped into my path as I reached for the door handle. I measured him and decided two blows. That mother is too big to screw around with. I'll finish it fast.

I recognized his kind right away, accustomed to intimidating people with his size. The son of a bitch was totally unprepared when the tip of my boot connected with his balls. His face screwed up, into a grimace—rage smothered by pain. It appeared on his face like a toothy, childish smile. My right hook sent him to the pavement. He dozed in a pool of his own vomit. I saw the cops out of the corner of one eye just as the first brick smashed the windshield of the hearse; the crowd started yelling, pressing me against the hearse. It seemed red-face had some friends. One moment business type surrounded me, the next I was shielding my face from punches and flying glass.

I can't recall the blow that knocked me to the pavement but my face rested just inches from a big red, pitted mess of drool.

The kicks to my ribs turned everything black for a moment. When I heard the gunshots, I thought, oh shit. But seconds later there I was standing, no pain anywhere. Two cops held me upright, their guns drawn. Sirens, the screeching tires. The crowd was backing off.

It took me awhile to focus. The windshield on the hearse was gone. Glass was everywhere; two other squad cars stood by with blue lights flashing. Two cops stuffed me in the back seat of a squad car. I looked out the window and all I could think was, oh my god! The hearse with Ben's body stood there like a wasted derelict, windows broken, tires flat. I bowed my head and tears came as the cop car drove away with me in the back seat.

Judge Mead seemed an amiable old man. The charges against me were read by that little asshole from the county attorney's office: public drunkenness, driving under the influence, disturbing the peace, assault and battery, causing a riot. I tried to explain that none of this was my fault, the judge told me to shut up, sit and listen. Your lawyer will plead your case. And the list of charges continued to grow. After awhile, I felt compelled to say something in my own defense because you were saying nothing, Oscar. Again, the judge told me to shut up, sit.

Well, no one patronizes me. I certainly gave the old fart a piece of my mind, didn't I? Castigated the old son of a bitch. How was I to know that red-face was his son?

But firing you was a stupid move. Nothing of importance happened after you left. Guess you didn't want to see me make an ass of myself huh? I presented my defense against all charges. When I was through the judge looked me straight in the eyes, shook his head from left to right, and a little crafty smile appeared on his face.

"Are you finished?"

"Yes sir."

"I was rather tolerant with you today. I allowed you to go off at the mouth, hoping that you would absolve yourself but you took it too far. All charges against you are dropped, Mr. Loveless. But I am committing you to a psychiatric ward. You will stay there until a doctor says it's okay to release you. Your choice of words to address this court shows a definite lack of restraint. I should throw you in the county jail but I don't think that would do you any good. Maybe this will teach you how to control that tongue. Good day, Mr. Slaughter."

He got up and walked out. You told me the man was famous for exacting bizarre sentences. But this? So Oscar, help me out here. Look this over; tell me how much to tell them. I know if I told them all this it could be quite frightening. I don't want to be pushed any further. As you know, if my back is against the wall I'll fight.

Sincerely,
Jeremiah Slaughter.

Dear Jerry,

Don't be surprised at my tone. I'm in my office with my tie loose, my jacket off, a shot of whisky and a cool beer before me. I'll be heading home soon. Why am I thinking of you? You are possibly the stupidest son of a bitch I have ever had to represent in a court of law. The next time you find yourself before a judge, sit quietly and let your attorney do his job. What the hell did you think you hired me for?

When you are finished reading this letter burn it. I have full intentions of rising to the highest office that this, my chosen profession, will allow. I don't want this surfacing to haunt me. In your letter, you speak of truth. There's little truth in a court of law. There is a stripped version, stripped of all its subjectivity. It stands there like a woman naked in a crowd with one hand across her breast and the other covering her pubic area. We call it facts. Did you know that fact and truth are two different entities entirely?

I thought of not responding to you at all, then I thought of an official thing on my office stationary, typed up by my secretary. All of those seemed woefully inadequate. The tone of your letter screamed for a personal response, but I don't know what to say. You are asking the wrong guy to comment on things of such a personal nature. You recall the first time Ben introduced us. I took one look at you and thought, now there's a powder keg ready to blow with the first spark. You seemed to carry the race thing on your sleeve. I have a different view of you now.

We have a few things in common. There was also a time in my life when I couldn't see the light, and I too have a certain lack of respect for judges, the police and even some lawyers. You know that joke about God and an angel looking down on a boat sunk in sharks infested waters. The sharks circled, picking off people one by one. When they came to the last guy, a lawyer, they swam up to him and just gave him a bump. "What was that?" The angel asked God. "Professional courtesy," God replied. I always laugh at that joke because I see the inherent misunderstanding. Lawyers are of two kinds: Prosecutors and defense. I prefer the defense side. Police and judges are the enemy. Did you know that more than 90% of judges were once prosecutors? In my profession we call that the unholy alliance. The judges sit up there in their robes like hallowed priests. You know why judges wear robes. A left over from when priests did the job of judges.

I assume you are familiar with that period in history when the church ran every-one's life. They told men and women, when and how to screw, they doled out penalties for masturbation, and if anyone opened their mouth in protest or pretense of intellectual propriety they were instantly branded a heretic and burned at the stake or tortured to death in some dark, wet dungeon.

I don't know why I'm rambling on about such rubbish. You want to know how to get out of that forensic unit. Don't worry about it. They can only hold you for thirty days, and after that, they have to show cause why you should still be held. Stall; don't give them anything to use against you. Relax; enjoy the free room and board. If you have to write for them, use material from way back in your life, when you were a boy, before your mother killed your father. In three weeks, I'll petition the court and you'll be out of there.

This is all pro bono. The next time you see me around, buy me a couple beers. And stay out of the battles you can't win. There is always that time when silence becomes the savior. We call it pleading the fifth. Enjoy the vacation. You earned it.

Oscar Peterson.

FAR FROM SHORE

My Name is Alfred Saint Giles. I'm a fisherman from the island of Grenada. My boat capsized in a squall three days ago. So much water and nothing to drink. By day, I'm roasting in this silver-blue heat. My legs went numb sometime last night. My tongue is like a stone in my throat. I can hardly feel my other parts. Drink your belly full of this seawater and say goodbye, Saint Giles. But my brain refuses to obey. It's grasping at thoughts about a man who went through this exact experience and lived to tell the tale. We called him Uncle Orisha.

I was twelve years old when my attention focused on him. Some of the other fishermen came up with this game. The stake was twenty dollars. Laugh the longest and you get the money. Uncle Orisha laughed for over one hour without stopping for water, and before he was finished, everyone near him was laughing uncontrollably. He was not my uncle. He was the grandfather of my friends Wilfred and Marcus Dabreo. I never understood why everyone called him Uncle Orisha.

Like a fishhook, the man was long and curved, a perfect fit to the sea. He regarded the water the way some men regarded the land. He spoke of his work out there with reverence, as if coupled to all of it. *'First, you bait the shaft of the hook. Drop it down into the water and watch the tide take it. Gently cradle the cord across these two fingers, pare out the line. Not all at once. Keep the slack out; wait for the bite'.* That's how the man who was named for the Yoruba's 'God of the head' gave tongue to the work he did.

I heard him another time as he spoke to Marcus and Wilfred. We had plans to go spin our tops and play some marbles that day. School was out for Christmas. Uncle Orisha must have been talking to the guys long before I came along, because they both glanced at me with these funny looks on their faces. The man was speaking words that made no sense at first. It took me several seconds to catch on: *"...it was all part of this island and this sea",* he was saying. *"I had to learn it. My father said so. In those days, we listened to our parents. The first time he dipped me into the sea, it went into my mouth and came out of my nose. I coughed and coughed, then I could breathe again. I filled my lungs with air and as I breathe out, I knew it. I relaxed with the water, a baptism to the Almighty Sea-god that keeps us all right here, on this rock, in the middle of this ocean. This creature that feeds us, waiting, calm and flat, remembering everything. But when you least expect it. Wham! Payday. Don't ever take the sea for granted, you hear me. Now go play."* And he waved us off with a hand that looked like claws.

Uncle orisha's wife, Miz Louisa, she didn't come

out with food that day. Their house was my favorite place to go. Miz Louisa was a baker. She always fed us warm slices of bread with butter, chunks of sponge cake that melted in my mouth. And sometimes sorrel or ginger beer to wash it down. This woman, her house, what she did with flour, shorting and yeast. Stupid memories. The water is cold. Thirst is bad but hunger is gnawing.

I never should have become a fisherman. Farming could have been a reasonable profession. Now I may never fall in love or have children. After my father is dead, who will say a prayer for me on Fisherman's Birthday? Who will drop a wreath into the sea for me, from that beach of black sand?

Would I ever see that sand again? I would give anything to be there right now, hauling this boat out of the water, getting ready to go down to the rum shop for a nip. If I survive this, I'll marry the first woman who would have me, I'll have many fat children. I'll learn a trade, one that keeps my feet on the land. Uncle Orisha, can I be as lucky as him? Will this sea give me back to the land? And what's the use, in the end the sea took him anyway.

I heard things said about that man. Other jealous fishermen would go on with words like these: *"That Orisha, he must be dealing with the sea devil. How can he be the only one to go out and come back with his boat full of fish, up to both gunwales, all the time? And look at what happened to Diggs. I'm telling you!"*

Diggs Masanto. My grandfather, Uncle Orisha's fishing partner. One day they left Black Bay for their usual deal with the sea. It took Uncle Orisha six weeks to return and he returned alone. A vessel from Venezuela dropped him off on the wharf in Saint Georges one night. He came walking up the road to his house, in the dark, with only the clothes on his back. His wife fainted when she saw him standing in the doorway.

The next day he spoke to my father, telling him about the last days of my grandfather's life. Seventy-two hours they spent hanging on the gunwale of the capsized boat. The promises made. A day after Grandpa Diggs slid under the waves, three Venezuelan whiskey smugglers stumbled on Uncle Orisha. They hauled him out of the sea and took him to a town called La Salinas, on the eastern edge of Venezuela, near Trinidad. They were all arrested as they attempted to unload the cargo of smuggled whiskey.

No one in La Salinas spoke English, so Uncle Orisha was thrown in jail along with the smugglers. It took a whole month before a priest who spoke English visited the jail. Uncle Orisha was released after the priest translated for him. And it took him two more weeks before he could find a boat that would allow him to work his way back to Grenada.

Uncle Orisha and my father became father and son after that. But he refused to take my father as a partner on his new boat. He claimed he couldn't shoulder any more promises or stand to see another man drown. So, my father took a job at the sugar factory in Woburn. In reality, no one else wanted to fish with Uncle Orisha. So, he fished alone.

One morning on my way to school, I saw Uncle Orisha preparing his boat for a day on the water. He was starting late. All the other boats were long gone.

I came up behind him silently. He turned and looked at me as my shoes scuffed the ground. "Alfred, never creep up on a man like that. What you doing so far behind? You going to be late for school."

"Good morning, Uncle Orisha," I replied. Not knowing what else to say. I started running fast to catch my friends. But I watched as he rowed past the point that stuck out into the ocean like a finger, and hoisted his sail. That was the last time any of us saw him. He didn't return from the sea that day.

Uncle Orisha was a very lucky man. He got many chances. Twice before, he had run into problems on the sea and he was rescued. Once by what I would call a miracle, but this time they found nothing, neither him nor the boat. That was over twelve years ago. Quite amazing how these figments inhabited my reality, contributing to me being out here, floating around with little chance of rescue. Uncle Orisha and his many stories, each one gave me a chill the first time I heard him tell it.

I have no idea how old he might have been when I heard him speak that night. He was telling us about his second rescue. In my young eyes, he was ancient and legendary. He had sprinkles of gray hair around the fringe of his head, near his ears and in the short beard on his chin. He sat before some of his friends trying to explain how he managed to be on the beach near Glover Island when they found his boat capsized miles out at sea. No one could have swum that distance against the tide.

Uncle Orisha looked right and proper as he grappled with some words trying to explain. It took him awhile to get to the meat of the story. Everybody came, friends and backbiters, loitering in his yard, near the brick oven that his wife, Miz Louisa, used to bake her delicious Tight-breads. This was an occasion. Everyone who knew him came out.

His daughter Sybil with her two children, Wilfred and Marcus nestled at his feet. His wife, miz Louisa, she sat so close to him it looked as though she wanted to crawl into his skin. They all gathered around him, his son, Norbert, my father Ethan. This group formed the first circle around Uncle Orisha. Others skulked just beyond the range of the light cast by the torch made from a Fanta bottle, a rag for a wick, and kerosene.

An owl hooted from its perch out in the branches of the old silk cotton tree. I waited with the others. We wanted to hear Uncle Orisha confirm the rumors that were going around. We watched him as he ate the Oildown. First with a spoon, then with his fingers, picking up the chunks of breadfruits and pig-snouts covered with callaloo.

He kept licking his fingers. He spoke with his mouth half full, chewing the words and the food. The man told us of the blue sky and the blue water, how they slid into each other. No horizons. Impossible to tell where one ended and the other began. Uncle Orisha spoke about the motion of the waves, how they moved under his boat, taking it up to the peaks, then gently down into the troughs. Finally, his words drifted into the part I wanted to hear:

"Ever notice? Just before rain, how the fish starts biting. Almost jumping on the hook. I saw the weather, but the fishes were biting so good. Then wham, just like

that." He gestured over his head with one hand. *"The squall fell out of the cloud, right on top of me. It was as if God sneezed, and a hole opened in the sky. The rain and wind beat my skin raw. Tossed the boat around. Before I could react, the boat flipped over. I came up coughing water and snatching for the gunwale, trying to catch my breath. Waves lashed, foams flying. Finally, I grabbed on. The squall lasted over fifteen minutes, then it was gone. I looked around, couldn't tell up from down. No land anywhere in sight. I swear, night came with the wind and rain. I could barely make out chunks of gray cloud drifting far across the horizon. All that water and darkness coming.*

"I hugged the boat tight, fagged out and scared. Little voices were telling me, all you have to do is hold on. Hold on. Someone. A cargo vessel, those Venezuelan whiskey smugglers. What would they think if the same fellows found me again? Would they leave me behind, thinking that I'm some kind of ghost, some kind of Flying Dutchman?" **Uncle Orisha** laughed that laugh that echoed from his throat instead of his mouth, then he continued.

"Stars came out and the moon moved across the sky. I imagined some of you feeding wood to a big fire on the beach, warning passing ships about me out there. Sometime, toward morning, my joints turned to jelly. It was as if I had no skin and the sea was washing my bones. I was nodding off when I felt something brush across my ribs. I came alert quickly, my heart pounding like a drum. Sharks. Oh, shit! Sharks. So, this is it? It all ends here. Not like this. O'lord. I started to pray. And I waited for the first hit to bust my guts wide open,

turn the water red. They would drag me down, ripping me apart like bait." He hesitated and looked out at us as if searching for some kind of reaction. Ever now, as I'm floating here, I can see his face and how his words come up to us that night, mixed with the stench of kerosene smoke.

"Nothing happened," he continued *"I opened my eyes slowly. One at a time. My teeth still clenched tight as a vice. They kept circling, diving under the boat. My heart slowed when I noticed it was only a big school of porpoises. They were making strange noises like a flock of birds. It sounded like a conversation.*

"A big one came up close and looked at me with huge glossy eyes, black and shallow as a cows' eyes. I saw pity in those eyes. Then it turned and swam right between my legs, snuggled itself into my crotch and tugged forward. It made that noise again and I could feel it vibrate up into my loins. The boat lay on its side, but it was so much better than the back of that fish. The porpoise tugged forward again and made that noise. What can it be saying? Are they reading the beats of my heart? My heart had to be speaking to them? Finally, I did let go, but I still couldn't stop thinking that this could be a joke on me. So many porpoises I killed, ate and sold. What if this fish heave me off; leave me floating miles from shore. The back of the creature was smooth as a baby's backside. I had to struggle to stay on.

"The school swam with me for a long time. They bunched up to keep me steady. They swam in near Glover Island. They waited for me to crawl ashore, then they turned back to sea and headed north. I swear,

never, never catching or eating another porpoise as long as I live. And if any of you catch one and bring it ashore, I swear, I'll kill you."

The crowd clapped their hands and laughed. Uncle Orisha was looking at us as if he wanted to say more, but he said nothing else. A strange expression lingered on his face. To this day, I'm sure that he was serious about the threat to kill anyone who harmed a porpoise.

For many years after Uncle Orisha was gone, I expected him to return. I looked forward to him just appearing one day and blessing us with another of his fantastic tales about what happened to him out there, who rescued him and where they took him that time.

However, as the years went by, my confidence in that happening withered and I started imagining what truly may have happened to him. Now I too am a fisherman in the same situation. I am waiting to be rescued, or waiting for my strength to run out. One or the other will happen. If it comes to pass that the sea should claim me, I'll laugh. I'll laugh that giddy laugh, just as I imagined Uncle Orisha would have done as he slid under the waves and became one with this Atlantic ocean that never forgets and seldom forgives.

BEAT ME

If they knew my true crime, they wouldn't be so kind to me. I'll try to keep this brief. I don't have to try to fool you. At first I thought, I'll tear my clothes into strips, make a rope, throw it over that grate in the window and place the noose around my neck. That will be that. I'll save myself from the humiliation that lay ahead. I'll save the State some money, save my parents from the pain of having to worry about my existence. They shouldn't have made me their only child. They should have adopted one or two more, give themselves a little leeway incase one of us turned out to be a pitiful disappointment. But then, this other choice turn out to be more salient because of its proposal by the liar and the cheat.

I was nineteen when my girlfriend, Heather told me she was pregnant. I should have paid closer attention to the way she phrased that announcement. An abortion was possible, but out of reach. I would have to bag lots of groceries to get the cash. Asking my parents for the money to get my girlfriend and abortion? Out of the question. Marrying her seemed easier. I told myself I'll put off college for a couple years. Go fulltime at the store. The plan looked good. Heather looked me in the eyes, smiled, and agreed to this composition of our life.

Stupidity should be a crime. People should be jailed for being stupid. If that were so, I wouldn't have had the chance to make a mess of things. The stupid squad would have burst down my door with guns drawn: "Mitch, you have been declared an idiot and must go to jail, they would said. "We fear you might foul up the universe. Your wife Heather informed on you."

Heather and I slid gently into marital life. Her family and mine were happy to leave us alone. My father gave me one piece of advice. Boy, he said, *don't get burdened by too many children. Don't fuck yourself into poverty.*

After the birth of Tag, she cried for three weeks straight. She would be in tears when I left for work and still be crying when I got back. That was sheer hell, looking at her puffy face and those swollen red eyes, unable to do anything. Her mother and mine called it postpartum depression. One day I came home and all that was gone. We crawled into bed and sex took on a distinct dimension. She coiled herself around me, she helix and curled, she licked me with an electric tongue. We did things that I had only seen in porn films. I appreciated her efforts immensely.

Her breasts had grown from her pregnancy and they remained luxurious, cushioned and musky. She maintained a little plumpness on her body, and that made her look a little like her mother. You know those women with a stout body and a good-looking face. She turned into that sort of woman in nine months. Not giving her what she wanted was out of the question. So, two years later the second boy, Demo was born.

Tag and Demo. Heather insisted on those names. She said her name was too ordinary. Thinking of her now, her name should have been Rose, beautiful but with thorns, sharp enough to draw blood. As the boys grew, people would frequently inquire about their real names and I would have to explain. My mother, the plain speaking washer-woman, she once declared that those were wonderful names for dogs, not children.

Tag was two years old the year Kenneth Moore came back to Noblesville. There was a rash of robberies and an attempted rape that year. This prompted me to buy a gun and teach Heather how to shoot. Ken was an old friend and schoolmate. One of the people voted most likely to succeed in our crop of farm boys, town boys, and jocks. The rumors that Ken had gotten into drugs out in Los Angeles didn't prevent us from inviting him over for dinner.

Heather was not her usual self that night. She acted jittery and asked Ken a few lackluster questions. Did he ever go to acting school as planned? Did he ever get married or have children? We spoke about people we knew. The ones who went to Chicago and came back six months later, the ones who found religion, those who vanished into the American masses and was never heard from. At one point Ken started telling us about his sexual encounter with a well-known older actress. Heather stood up and said, "what a waste." She left the room and never returned. I was relieved when he left our house that night. She refused to discuss that night, or her eruption of rudeness.

When we heard that Ken was arrested at a storage unit in Carmel, loading all the stuff he had stolen from people in our town into a truck, we were surprised. He received ten years in prison. The fool should be out by now with good behavior.

I received my promotions at the grocery store not so much for my hard work, but through the social activities of Heather. She would cook and invite my bosses with their wives to dine with us frequently. She had a way of flirting that made men feel singular and women unthreatened. Heather arranged her hair in a manner reminiscent of television mothers from the fifties. She even wore those aprons with frills. I must admit those aprons actually turned me on. We bought a house with the extra money I made from my promotion to manager. Truly amazing, time does have wings.

The phone calls started one morning, and continued for over a month. At first, I simply ignored the caller, then, I threatened to call the police. Who's this fool talking about the paternity of my children? I must say her persistence actually wore me down, because I started looking for guarantees in the features of the children.

One time she called and I lost it. She sounded as if her mouth was full of food. "You talking to me with your mouth full?" I shouted at her. "You eating? What kind of freak are you? You must be some fat, bored. . . You doing this because I work at a grocery store?" She hung up the phone without answering or saying another word. But the next day she was back. "Don't you think they should have inherited some of your complexion?" She asked the question, then waited for an answer. This time I hang up.

At my dentist's office two days later, in a magazine called Popular Science, I stumbled on an article about genetic testing. The newest tools use by police to track down criminals. The piece looked like a God send. Reflecting on all this now, I realize it must have been the devil not God. I should have left it alone and continue to live in ignorance. The cliché about ignorance and bliss does contain a definite ring of truth.

The signs were all there. Heather had this air of looking down on me. Nothing overt, no public displays, but I could tell by the way she phrased certain things, little corrections. She was the only girl at our school who was on the debate team and ran for Homecoming Queen at the same time. She lost by two votes to a girl who would later go on to win the beauty contest known as the Pork Queen Of Tipton County. I was not the kind of guy that girls flocked to. So, when Heather showed me some attention and started having regular sex with me, I was hooked. I must admit to an immense pride in the association.

But on the other hand, I'm amazed at how some people would talk. Some of them even had the nerves to ask me to my face: "what are you?" The complexion of my skin became a favorite topic of conversation for some. You see I have a tan that remains all year round. I have no knowledge of my ancestry. It could be Jewish, Mexican, Black, Arab or Italian. It never mattered to me. I've always thought of myself as a white man who tans easily.

Marrying a girl like Heather should have been the beginning of great things for me. There was only one drawback. She always sidestepped the issue of finding a job. She would ask me if I would like to see my wife toiling like my parents. My father is a janitor and my mother works at the laundry in a hotel. Ordinary folks. They bowled three nights a week and often drank too much beer. She had the nerve to insult these two decent people, and I just sat there and took it.

At first, the woman's voice on the other end of the phone was disguised and barely audible, but it grew in authority with each call. She said a different thing each time as if reading from a prepared script. But it always came back to checking the paternity of the children, then she would hang-up. I tried to ignore the whole thing, but her hints kept eating at me. These were suggestions that I just couldn't ignore.

Women are always sure, I told myself. They carry the children in their stomachs. Beyond trust, how can men ever be sure? I moved to ease the strain on my ego. The woman called one morning, and I decided to play the game, disarm that fool with science. I had seen that shit on Jerry Springer and other television shows, read that article in the magazine. Lord have mercy, the stuff I set in motion.

I was amazed at the ease. Little swabs of cotton on the insides of the mouths of Tag and Demo. I did the same for me and placed it in a container specially marked. Then I posted the kit to a lab in Indianapolis. It took two weeks for me to get the results. I remember some key words from the sheet of paper they sent me. Presumed father excluded; probability of paternity zero. I called a number on the piece of paper and spoke to a fellow for fifteen minutes. The outcome felt like a snake in my guts. "Yes, do it again," I told him.

Heather sat at the kitchen table and I sat across from her. Her head was down, hanging over the second set of results. I know she wasn't reading it. She didn't touch it. It rested on the table. I could hear the voice of the two boys romping in the living room. We frequently screamed at them for playing rough in the house. Two words came out of her mouth. No hint of regret, sorrow or apology.

"What now?" She said.

It was more of a statement, than a question. The words struck me and left an essence, a kind of swelling in the center of my chest that forced me to complete a quadruple of stupid words.

"Who is it, Heather?"

"That's not important, Mitchell." She looked up at me and almost whispered the last part. "I'm not telling you that."

She had this way of seizing a situation. Making it hers, as if she was the last arbiter. The nerve of that bitch? Trying to tell me what's important. All the joys of the two children crumbled into the hushed miracle of her last words. I wanted to punch her in the face, shout down her throat at what ever might be inside of her. You bitch, you have the nerve to refuse me. But a scornful conclusion kept me silent and stock-still. It was the voice of a judge awarding all my property to Heather because I made her face look like ground beef.

"You are the presumed father, Mister Stock," the judge was saying in my head. *"These children were born into your household while you were married to their mother. You will have to pay child support until they are eighteen, regardless of that test. And since she will have custody of the children, I'll have to give her the*

house. Sorry Mister Stock, like it or not, that is the law. Our goal here is the welfare of the children."

"Anything to do with the color of my skin, Heather?"

A nervous little snigger escaped her lips. I thought I saw this crack in the veneer of the porcelain bitch.

"Your complexion is your best attribute, Mitchell." She looked up at me. Something that seemed to be a smile flashed across her face.

"You treat me like a nigger and now you…you going to tell me how much you love me?"

"I read this once, on a bathroom wall: *our lives are shaped by those who love us and by those who refuse to love us.* Would you like some tea?" She stood up and moved to the stove.

I'll be working two days of every week to support these kids. I could hear the voice of my father echoing in my head, *Boy, don't fuck yourself into poverty.* I'll drive by this house and imagine her crawling into bed with other men. How many people in this town know? Will I be forever suspicious of laughter, the kind heard as I walk around the store, pretending to be the man in charge? The clothing I wore to work suddenly took on the resemblance of a clown's costume.

"You are quoting me platitudes from shit-house walls. So, what do you suggest, Heather?" Panic gripped me the moment those words left my mouth.

We sat in silence. She looked as if thinking. A car horn honked on the street outside. No one will ever respect me here. Never again. Did they ever? The end to all this came to me in a blinding flash. I stood up from the table and walked into the living room where I kept the gun on a high shelf near the door. *Is it easier to shoot a child in the back?* The thought flashed through my head as I pointed the gun at the boys and pulled the trigger twice. Click, click.

Nothing happened. They didn't even notice what I did. They were laughing, playing a video game, paying zero attention to me. Heather came up behind me; she reached out and took the gun out of my hand. I stood there, stiff. The outcome of what I had attempted to do drained me.

"Boys, boys," she spoke softly.

Tag and Demo looked up at her standing next to me, the gun concealed behind her back. "Go on down to your grandmother's house and stay there until I come for you." The words came out of her mouth, calm, matter of fact. "Go on," she said. They both appeared a little confused and resistant.

"But mom," they both protested in unison, "the game."

"Do as I say. You hear me?" She raised her voice.

The two boys shuffled around, collected a few things, their backpacks, stuff two walk-mans, one into each pack. They headed for the door reluctantly. The screen door creaked on the hinges and it slammed back against the jam. I should fix that, I thought, and the inanity of it struck me, the silence left behind by the departure of the two boys, the vacuousness of my whole life.

I was trying my best to fight off something combustible inside of me. I felt hot, as if a fever was burning its way out of me through the top of my head. "Come into the kitchen," she said, still holding the gun. She seemed to have complete control of the situation. I just wanted to wake up and realize that all this was just a bad dream.

So, I followed her into the kitchen. "It would be a shame to mess up that nice carpet," she said.

We sat down at the table and she methodically loaded six bullets into the gun as the kettle whistled on the stove, then she placed it near my hand. "If you need to kill something," she made a little gesture with her hand, "kill me," She stood and poured two cups of tea. "Before you do it, let me clear something up. I never told you that Tag was your child. I told you I was pregnant, you assumed and I said nothing. You were my savior, Mitchell. How could I refuse?" She paused and shrugged her shoulders. The gesture irritated me. "Demo was a stupid mistake," she said. "I just wanted to feel..." She hesitated for a moment. "I'm not going there. I'll be stealing more from you. That was never my intention. I always wanted this family to be . . . This thing was killing me, Mitchell. I wanted to tell you so... a few times it hang off my bottom lip; my brain refused . . . Praise God this is out."

"Out where? A woman called me a number of times."

"I know," she said. "I hired her."

Heather was looking straight at me with a mixture of audacity and smugness on her face. The sheen of beauty I once saw around her vanished. She looked like a boil. Fat ass, a protuberance of nasty flesh perched on a chair.

"I need to cry, Mitchell. I've shed no tears since the birth of Tag. Beat me, Mitchell. Beat me," she said. "Do anything to me if it'll keep us together. I surrender. I'll be anything you want. Just don't go. Don't make me go." The words came out of her mouth and they made me furious. If there were tears with her word, they would have struck me different. The way it hit me, her proposal sounded like a bribe. In that instant, something happened to me. I saw an image of broken glass, fallen down and scattering.

"Why did you do it? Hire that woman to call me. What for?"

"You know, Mitchell. Doctors have this procedure. When you have an ulcer, they cut out the distress flesh. Allowing the new wound to heal."

She flinched when I stood up and snatched the gun off the table. I dashed outside, stood in my front yard and pointed the weapon at the sky, emptying all six bullets into the air. I should have killed her, I thought. How could she know that I would be so spineless? Must be amazing what you can learn about a person after living with them for over ten years.

It took the police five minutes to come and arrest me. They came with guns drawn. They handcuffed me and placed me in the car, then they went into the house and spoke to Heather. One uniformed guy came back and started lecturing me about the damage a bullet can cause just falling back to earth. I guess she didn't tell them about me pointing the gun at the kids. I'm thankful to her for that. The car drove away, and I looked back at her standing on the porch. I couldn't help but wonder if she could fulfill that beastly proposal.

THE VISITOR

I'm standing at my kitchen window, looking into the dispersion of light across the road. It's late. Twelve thirty, I would say. I bought this small house after the incident. All the structures here are strictly functional, totally lacking architectural artistry. The small blue house on the other side of the road from where I live captivated my attention. On the first night, it was the blue light of the television screen glowing through the sheer curtain on the plate glass window. But in the light of day, it was the multiple signs on the front door: NO PEDDLERS, NO SOLICITORS, OXYGEN IN USE, NO SMOKING.

I've been living here for about one month and have been in contact with the inhabitant of that house just once. Going out to my car last week, I saw a genderless specter with face, and neck as white as milk. No other part of the body showed. The person was fully clothed down to white gloves on both hands. It stared me down hard, then slipped around the side of the house like a cat.

Had this person heard of me, or seen me on that television set that glowed blue at night? I was accused of a particular viciousness. What would it be like to do such a thing? The particulars that compose such mania. I have nothing like that in me. Take for instance, the events that triggered this stage of my malignancy.

I had seen this guy in the bars around town several times. He was reserved, although clothed in the latest gear. The fellow was engaging the people around him with no bravado. Just my type, and that mustache, I was sure it would tickle. I walked up to him one evening and introduced myself. He was sitting at the bar in a French restaurant down town called Millicent's. That was not my style, not the kind of thing that I usually do, but I found the guts that time. He looked depressed. I was hoping to cheer him up and turn him into the right company.

"I'm Robin," I said, offering him my hand.

"Oh! Hi," he said, I'm Harold Fletcher. He took my hand without standing.

He was dressed in an understated way, differently than his usual bar garb. His hand felt soft and small like a child's. He looked me up and down with attentive eyes, but his lips told another story. My friend Stanley once warned me about this kind of guy, the ones who introduce themselves using both their names.

The whole thing between Harold and I happened quickly. We had drinks and dinner, then went back to my place that night. After we made love, he simply excused himself, refused to spend the night. This went on for a month. What kind of a fool am I, I started thinking, getting involved with a man who might be married or somehow involved? When he finally invited me to his house for dinner, I was floored. He lived with his seventy seven year old mother in a nice, big house. I felt embarrassed about having taken him to the seamy room where I lived.

The complexities between Harold and his mother, Donna, I should have grasped after the first dinner. Nothing as explicit as strained words, but there was static in the air. I attributed this to my residual feelings about the condition under which I left the home where I was raised. Imagine people who once loved you asking you to leave and never return?

When Harold and Donna invited me to rent one of the rooms in their house, I was divided. What does she think is the relationship between Harold and me? We would have total privacy on the top floor he told me. His mother never came up there. He said he had set many traps to see if she crawled up the stair to have a look at his things when he was out. Not one of the traps was ever sprung. He claimed that Donna hadn't been on the top floor of the house since the death of his father. Harold said he needed time to clarify our relationship to her.

I shouldn't have taken his word. I should have asked more questions, insisted on certain things, but I was giddy about Harold and the stability that he represented. I even started fantasizing about what life might be like with him and me after Donna was out of the picture. She had to die eventually.

About three month after moving in, Harold and I were lounging in bed after making love. I was dozing in his embrace, meditating on this occasion of his satin hands sending chills through me. Oh, the sweetness that came to pass. There was a noise and Harold jumped up. I looked around and saw Donna standing in the doorway.

The old woman screamed as if she had seen the devil himself. She turned from us and I could hear her muttering as she went down the stairs. Harold rushed out of the room, bare-assed like a little boy. I got dressed and hurried to his room. I wanted to know why he hadn't explained us to his mother. How could she not recognize that her son was gay? After all, they say mothers are the first to know.

Harold was gone. It seemed he had gotten into his clothes and fled. Down stairs, I found Donna sitting on the couch. Her eyes were red. Her makeup smeared down her face. Her frosted hair in a mess. She held a kerchief with both hands. "What have you done to my son, you pervert?" She asked.

"Donna, Harold is a grown man. He's just gay. I didn't do anything to him." I wanted to kill Harold for leaving me here with her.

"Turned him into a. . ." she sniffled. "Get out of my house. You rapist, get out. You raped my son."

I decided to walk away, then I ran. I hope this was not the end of my newfound joy, but I'm going to kill Harold when I see him. Son of a bitch. I was gone for about twenty minutes when I discovered that I had fled without my wallet.

When I got back to the house, a police car was parked at the curb. I had a strange inclination to just turn and bolt, but I decided I had done nothing wrong. Why should I run? I walked into the house. Donna sat on the couch with her handkerchief wadded in one hand. She pointed to me with one bony finger, a horror stricken look in her eyes, her lips quivered. Two policemen rushed me and threw me hard to the floor. I could feel and hear my shoulders creak as they forced my hands behind my back and handcuffed them.

I looked at Donna, she was avoiding my eyes and looking at the cops as if pleading with them to do some deed that she dare not mention. I almost pissed my pants. I've heard stories of things happening to people like me in the custody of such brutes. They stuffed me into the backseat of the car like a piece of rag. Halfway down the road one of the cops started talking to me.

"What kind of a freak are you?" he asked as they drove me down to the station. "You get off on brutalizing old women? She's seventy-seven years old, man. Why did you have to rape her?"

I was amazed at the accusation. What could she have told them? Weeks later it came out that no rape had happened, but it seemed kind of a surprise to the local newspaper. They had run a story with a picture of me, the headline: MAN RAPES 77 YEAR-OLD WOMAN. The television stations ran stories about elder abuse for the next few days between commercials for new cars and trendy drugs that promise to prevent puckering of the lining of your esophagus and cure acid reflux disease.

Harold ran and hid like a scared cat. How can this gorgeous man of mine be such a coward? I actually expected him to come to my rescue. My feelings for him hardened. My friends told me to hire a lawyer. The man I hired was a troll who told disparaging stories about his profession. He acted like a doctor with bad bedside manners. He kept repeating the words injury and damages. I felt neither, after they had taken off the handcuff and released me from jail. But the fellow did his magic. He wrote a few letters and like an evil magician, he transferred money from the newspaper to me. No judge, no jury. Amazing how stuff that smells like shit can produce spuds. Would it be apt to say thank you to Harold? I used the money from the settlement to buy this house.

Now I'm standing here looking at the glow of that television set across the street and I know I finally comprehend what the lawyer meant. In times gone bye, I would have had no suspicions about the light colored truck pulling into the parking space in front of the small blue house. A man got out of the truck and walked up the few stairs to the front door. I'm sure he's not the person who lives there; the figure is lingering too long at the entrance. He came back down the stairs and stood in the yard for a moment. I glanced up and down the street to see if anyone might be coming. Witnesses, you know. When I looked again, the man appeared inside the house. Two silhouettes framed against the blue glow of the television, marionettes with no strings, arms gesturing threw the sheer curtains. Then they disappeared from view.

The next morning I'm standing at the window looking across the street and the truck is gone. A soft wind moved the yellow fall leaves across the grass. The knock on my front door startles me. I peeked through the shade and there stood the specter from across the street. It took me several seconds to summon up my wits, then I open the door.

"May I?" It was the voice of a woman. She spoke out of a mouth guarded by very red lips.

I stood back and pushed the screen-door open. Who the fuck are you, I was thinking. She rushed in as if fleeing from someone and stood there as I peeked outside, then closed the door behind us.

"I make the effort to meet all my neighbors, hello, how are you?" she said, unraveling the shawl from around her head, taking off her gloves, all in a hurry, as if she intended to stay awhile. Her pants were loose fitting like pajamas, her shirt hung long as a short dress and on her feet, she wore blue running shoes. She followed me into the kitchen. I felt uncomfortable with this person at my back. She took a seat without me offering. She had the features of a black woman but her skin was pasty white as if caked in powder. She looked vaguely familiar.

"I'm, Robin," I said.

"Lisher Saint Oinge." She spoke and we didn't shake hands.

"Lisher Saint Oinge is black." I'm looking at her as I say this and I realize it's foolish because now I recognize her. The woman that all my friends had on their walls in the dorms, some of them even took Farrar Fawcet down and replace her with Saint Oinge. Delicious Chocolate, they called her, and here she is sitting in my kitchen. The tabloids said she vanished just as she was about to ascend the throne as soft porn queen.

"You are spying on me, Robin."

"I'm just inquisitive."

"What's the difference?" She was looking at me as if waiting for an answer. "I recognize you the other day. From that awful news report."

"Aren't you afraid?"

"You don't look like a rapist, Robin. Actually, you are almost a swisher. I had lots of gay friends once."

Her frankness left warmth in the center of my chest. So, I smiled and said, "Who's spying on whom?"

She chuckled through red perfect lips, little fruit on a kabuki face. Hardly a smile. I should ask her the name of that shade. I should ask her who was her boyfriend who visited last night. After all, she introduced this lack of guile. Instead, I offered her food.

"I was just about to cook some breakfast," I said.

"Don't mean to be rude, but no thank you. I try to keep a strict diet with this skin, this vitiligo." She rubbed one hand across the skin on the other as if attempting to hug herself. "You know, at one time I wanted to be white." A little self-conscious smile darted across her face. "I know now, that being black or white is more than skin color." She paused and looked at me. "We should do dinner one night. We can go out, Dutch treat, or we can cook."

I felt sorry for her. Why would she want to have dinner with me? I wanted to ask her if the pigment had vanished from all of her body. But she stood and started wrapping her features into the shawl. "Cup of sugar or flour. Maybe you could use an egg sometime. Don't hesitate to knock, even if you are scared to have dinner with me."

She headed for the door with the same eruptive haste that brought her in. I watched her as she crossed the street and I wondered, will we be friends or just remain good neighbors?

WET STORAGE

I've been on the run, hiding from the law for almost two years. I've been told that I should get on a boat and head south, but Grenada is my home and I don't intend to leave. Some people are comparing me to Julian Fedor, but that is absurd. I do not intend to accept the yoke of history and carry it around like some jackass.

I keep hoping that the police will get tired of searching for me, but a kind of legend has grown around me, some true, some partly false. Egos have been bruised. Someday I expect someone in authority will try to put a bullet in my brain. But for now, this is it.

This began on a day in the middle of the wet season two years ago. Heavy rains fell out of a thick canopy of gray clouds hanging low over the valley we call, Mabimbay. Inside my thatched hut, I sat with only a kerosene torch for company. It had been raining for over an hour and I didn't expect it to cease anytime soon.

I'm usually a happy man, but that day I was indulging thoughts of death, of my father and all the others who pass on daily around here. Those who never got to leave this rock, people who sat near the shore gazing at the horizon and wondering. So many stories they take to the grave with them. It would be so good to catch and repeat all these, to my children, to anyone who would listen. I had no idea that my friend Ambrose was bringing news that would compel me to become a devout fraction of the chronicles of this rock and these people.

He came rushing out of the rain, flashing through the doorway like rushing water, his straw hat and khaki clothes dripping. He looked like a wet dog as he plopped down with his back against the bamboo ribs of the Jupa. Dirt from the floor clung to his wet clothing. Quite amazing what the mind preserves from crucial moments.

"We pray for it, but it's such a pain in the ass." Ambrose said.

The rain and wind was lashing the grass flat outside the hut. Thunder rolled now and then. I chuckled at his frustration with the weather. A soft mist blew through the doorway, causing the kerosene torch to dodge and flutter.

"So, this is the end," Ambrose said.

"What you mean by that?"

"You didn't hear, huh? Jacob and his brothers, they selling this whole place."

I looked at Ambrose and it was as if I had heard a peculiar and compelling tune. I had no idea that doubts hang on my face.

"You look as though you don't believe me, Ezekiel? Jacob will be driving pass any time now. He takes that road every day. Ask him." He spoke as if in defense of some article of faith, then he fell silent as if upset with me for doubting. The rain beat down outside. It was early evening, but it resembled the occasions called twilight.

The rain slackened to a slight drizzle and Ambrose left without divulging anymore. I decided to follow him before the rain start pouring again. I came down the hill onto the top road just as Jacob Elmo approached in his little jitney. I waved and he drove through a puddle of muddy water and pulled the vehicle to the side of the road near me. I plunged the fork into the ground, and leaned on it. The drizzle fell on my back, causing the shirt to cling to my skin.

"Hey Jacob, what you doing, man? I hear you planning to sell Mabimbay. Put me down for my three acres."

He gazed at me with a hollow expression that transformed into a look-warm smiled. "Ezekiel I wish I could do that," he said. "I start split it up into small pieces and each time I have to hire a surveyor. Selling it as one parcel is so much easier. And on top of that, we already have an offer from a firm in town."

I felt a chill unrelated to the light rain falling on my back. A firm. I knew it meant foreigners. What they call development. Large white houses and wire fences, paved roads, neatly cut grass and flower gardens. I had seen it before, in places like Grand Anse and Caliste. Where people once planted gardens, houses now sat on those spots.

"Jacob, lots of us work that land. We feed our children from that place. If we raise the money, would you . . .?"

"If you all can make us a comparable offer," he said.

"What you asking?"

"Hundred thousand." Jacob said the words and rolled up his lips as if he was certain that we couldn't come close to such a sum.

We were looking at each other and it was as if I saw Jacob for the first time. The son of a greedy pig turned into another greedy pig with no reverence for anyone else. The question of money and the land opened my eyes wide. Rainwater dribbled from my forehead in little streams. What do they call me behind my back, "A Briar Man"?

The man sat there on his ass in the jitney. I thought I knew him. He wore a beige business suit. His hair was neatly combed and oiled. There were no calluses on those hands resting on the steering wheel. His jitney, imported from some foreign country, stood idling on the side of the road. Could this be the same Jacob Elmo I once attended Grammar School with? I felt a sudden urge to grab him out of the vehicle and slam him into the mud, dirty up the son of a bitch.

"Can you guys raise that kind of money?" He asked the question and his eyes opened wide in a kind of faked surprise.

"I don't know about the others, Jacob. I've enough to buy my piece and the piece my father worked. I can get a mortgage."

"Sorry Ezekiel, we can't afford to break it up. That'll be so expensive. A tax every time we sell a piece. That new death tax is killing all of us," he laughed quickly. "Talk to the others. See what's what. Bring me something concrete."

He drove away in a hurry, almost running over my foot. I stood on that spot in the road for several seconds watching his jitney bump over the rough road. I was embarrassed, and outraged at the same time. Why am I begging?

People started calling me The Briar Man right after the death of my father. They called me this because they assumed that I was just like him, hard and rough. I inherited his reputation without striving one bit to earn it. I'm truly thankful for that portion of my inheritance. It serves me well these days.

Actually, I was once more of a jester. My favorite anecdote was about the land's reaction to my presence. Some people might say that they grew tired of hearing me tell that one, but I don't care. I'll tell it just this last time and no more. It goes like this: "After I eat my bakes and cocoa tea, I throw my fork on my shoulder and I head straight for my piece of ground. When she see me coming, she start to back, back, stumbling over herself, shouting 'Stop that man! Stop that man!' I walk up to her and plant my feet solidly; then she yields. All I have to do is just scratch her with my fork and she turns over, ready for planting." Most people laughed for so when I tell them that little fable. It has lost its flavor for me.

At home that evening, I found my wife, Alma cooking a fish stew and some white rice. The aroma of garlic and onions filled the kitchen. My two sons, Henry and James, were doing their homework on that table in the corner. They must be thankful to have that space all to themselves, now that their sister, Ruth is gone.

"Whose turn is it to bring back the milk in the morning, daddy, mines or Henry's?"

"Ezekiel, they have been quarreling about that all evening. They started the moment the rain came down. I told them you would settle it," Alma spoke and continued to stir the pot, not looking away from the food once.

"Henry, it's your turn," I said.

"I know, daddy."

"Then what's the argument about?"

"Nothing." He looked up at me with a sheepish grin, then turned back to the Caribbean Reader spread out on the table before him. That boy was always trying to get away with something.

We ate dinner and were listening to radio Six Ten from Trinidad, when I inquired about what they were reading in school.

"We're reading about the Caribs, daddy." James said. "Mighty warriors who threw their wives and children over Leaper's Hill instead of allowing them to become slaves." He spoke and I heard a certain reproach, as if I should be that kind of father.

"No brave and noble warriors would throw their wives and children to their death." The words leaped out of my mouth, a defensive reaction, and then it came to me. "That's like robbing your children of their inheritance, the opportunity to cut the throats of the oppressors one day. You see what I mean." I said it, then I felt a little accountable. So, I spoke quickly to cover. "A band of nasty white people must have gunned them down, dump their bodies over that precipice into the sea, and then makeup that ridicules story about the Caribs leaping to their death. Liars! Liars! All of them. They write that crap in books and feed it to you kids. If I had my way, you would stay away from that school. I know stories, better stories than they can cook up." Alma looked at me, shook her head and smiled without saying a word.

"Take Mabimbay for instance."

I was sitting there with a look on my face that said vex to James and Henry. But in reality, I was only searching for a way to make a convincing point. The boys appeared relieved that I was finish quarreling about the story in the schoolbook, and was about to tell them something about Mabimbay: "A giant come wandering across the world one day and stumbled on this rock in the ocean," I began. "It just happened to be lunchtime. The giant sat down; his butt rested on Mount Saint Catherine and his feet were stretched all the way down to Lance Aux Epine. He looked down at the ground right next to his knees. He brushed everything aside, lumping boulders and trees to form a surrounding ridge. What was left in his lap resembled a huge platter. The giant took food out of a big bag and had a belly-full. After the meal, he felt thirsty and began looking around for fresh water. Up on the ridge, between the trees, he spotted a place where a little water was trickling down between two rocks. He plunged his hand deep into the cleft and a torrent of water spouted up. Instantly, a river was born. The giant looked at what he had done and he liked it. He decided to give the place a name. He called it Mabimbay, after a place he had once seen in Africa."

The next morning Henry and I woke long before the first cocks crowed and headed up the hill to the garden and the cows. Every day, except Sundays, we made that trip, climbing the hill with my fork on my shoulder, my cutlass in one hand. The ocean, calm and blue, stretched out behind us, all the way to the imaginary.

My days went this way, milk the cow, and give Henry or his brother the pale to take home. Cut a couple bundles of grass for the cows. Fork some land, plant some provisions or pull out the big weeds. This is something that could take three hours or all day, depending on situations. I watched Henry as he left with the pale in one hand and a bag of mangoes in the other.

I've been laboring on that plot of land for many years. The river was still there, dividing the valley created by the giant. One half were cultivated with sugar cane, the other half were cultivated with plots of corn, pigeon peas, potatoes, yams, pumpkins and eddoes. These gardens belong to the men who cut and loaded the cane in the harvest season. Some of the food grown was kept to feed their families, and what's left were sold by wives and children in the marketplace in Saint Georges for cash.

My father, John Augustine, cultivated a piece of the same land before he died. He was the one who made the deal with Duncan Elmo, the father of Jacob, to pay the rent on the piece of ground in anyway he could. During a bad drought, many years ago, tempers were blazing high. Laquet, one of the oldest men still farming the valley, must have told this story a thousand times, and every time he told it, it grew in some way.

"They were young men then, chasing this woman called Monica. John Augustine seemed to be winning her over. Duncan hated this. He came to John one day about the rent on the ground. None of us had money. Nothing grew that year. They quarrel fiercely for a while, then the fight started, pushing and punching. Suddenly the cutlass came out. The blades clashed in midair and fell to the ground, two pieces. John and Duncan looked down at the shattered steel, and they started laughing loud. They realized how close they came to killing each other. From that day on they became very good friends."

I inherited the same deal as my father. Sometimes I paid the rent in cash and at other times, I paid it with a portion of my crops. Everything changed after the death of the two older men. My father died after a long illness. Some people claimed that one of his enemies must have worked "Obeah" on him. Jacob's father died about six months after mine. He was hardly in the grave before his kids announced that all rent on their land in the valley, from then on, would be paid in cash. No more old time deals.

The announcement didn't trouble me; I farmed the best piece of land in the valley and I worked hard. My plot was on a slope near the river and boundary with the cane. The fertilizer spread each year over the field would blow onto my land, enriching the already fertile soil. There were times that I dug yams and potatoes out of that ground. It took me hours and two men to carry one of them to market.

I've always enjoyed the comfort that having a little money can bring, and this comfort spread to all of my life. I knew the driving rainstorms that came whipping out of the hills--how cold and wet I felt, so many times as a boy helping my father with the crops and his cattle.

So, it wasn't long after I started gardening in Mabimbay that I built myself a jupa in the corner of my plot, right next to the cane fields. The grass around the jupa grew long and green. I cut it regularly and fed to my two cows. My jupa was the only shelter on that end of the valley. So, when it rained, all the other farmers came seeking shelter. That's how it came to pass that Ambrose was there with the news about the sale of Mabimbay.

Talking to Jacob had left me confused. I should have spoken to Alma, but I didn't want to trouble her with matters that she had no control over. I knew I should talk to T. A. Grenville, the leader of the labor union, but I was hesitant. I thought the family connection would make it look as though I was looking for special favors. You see, Grenville's son had married my daughter, Ruth and took her to England where he was attending law school. That morning, after Henry left with the milk, I decided that time shouldn't be wasted. After all, this concern was already in motion.

T.A. Grenville was a short, yellow man who looked as though he might come apart from something boiling in his belly. We called him the mongoose. He has been the leader of the labor movement in the district of Saint George for over twenty years. The man had led many strikes demanding more pay for the men who cut cane and work at the sugar factory. He had escaped many murder plots. If anyone could help, I knew he could.

Around lunch that day, I went to Grenville's house, intending to leave a message. My timing was good. His wife invited me to have lunch. We spoke about the importance of land. We ate a lunch consisting of fried bakes and codfish souse, washed it down with lime squash. Grenville agreed with me and promised to act as a go-between with Jacob. But we had to make some plans. Don't let the sun set on this, was what he said.

Later that day, he sent me a message, get the men together. I dispatched both my sons with messages, asking the other men to meet at my house that night.

They all came. Bottled torches supplied the light. Alma was kind of vexed with me for not telling her about all that. But she prepared some food and drinks for about fifteen men. Grenville spoke first, explaining to the gathering the role he would play. Promising his personal help, and the help of the labor union. Then it was my turn to speak to them. I spoke simply about what I had on my mind.

"Fellows, we all grew up together here with our parents and grandparents working that land. I don't know if any of you thought about it, but I thought about it hard. When I think about owning that piece of ground, I don't think about just me. I think about all of you and me, my children and yours. We need the land to plant. Our children will need it too. Through the union fund, a loan from Barclay's Bank and what money we have between us, we can buy half of Mabimbay and in the future, who knows, maybe even buy the cane fields. Working together, as a team, we can do this. We already work as some good teams when we have our maroons and fork each other's land. We know how to work together."

Silence fell on the little gathering as I stopped speaking. Grenville broke the silence from where he was standing. "Gentlemen," he said. "This is the chance of a lifetime. It's a chance to own your land, to work together, for yourselves. I found out something interesting. The Jacob and his family never owned Mabimbay. They are only caretakers. The land belongs to a company in England called Beck and Walters. I think if you want to buy the land you should communicate directly with the owners. I would be happy to be your representative in dealing with them."

Ambrose cleared his throat and came forward, speaking as he moved to the front of the crowd. "I don't have that kind of money and I don't want to get into debt. That land cost too much. There's so much that can go wrong. Remember that years when the rain didn't come?"

Groans and sighs spread through the gathering. They all seemed to converse in a hurried muddle of words. Laquet, the oldest man in the group, stood up and ambled forward. Ambrose yielded to the old man and stepped back. I was glad. I didn't need him throwing stones.

"Ezekiel, I worked that land many years with your father. You be just a little boy then. I'm an old man now. My wife passed on, my kids done grown and gone. I don't need that land no more, but I think you young fellows should buy it. It's good land. If I was you, I would buy all of it, even the cane. I'm with you, boy."

After Laquet, Atien spoke. I knew him to be practical and frugal. He was one of the people I was counting on most.

"I've some money saved, and I know that is good land. But what if I put my money in that land and no rain come? I know where I can get another piece of land. I don't need to give no white man in England my money. You all know how hard I work for my money, cutting cane, burning coals, selling provisions in the market. No way."

It seemed only the ones with no money wanted to buy the land, two young Rastas, that woman who refused to be a woman, all these on my side as long as I had the money. Finally, Ambrose spoke again, directly to me this time.

"Ezekiel, these are changing times. Men like us who work the land are dying out. Young folks don't want to work no ground. They're taking jobs in those hotels on the beach, on those yachts, going away to different countries. Look around, man. They can do whatever they want with that land. We can find other land to grow our provisions or get jobs."

He said the word job as if it was some kind of big punctuation mark on the end of a sentence. Only two words came to me. What then? That was all that came to my mind. What then?

The meeting ended just like that. I felt like an old bicycle tube that had picked up a nail. I had seriously misjudged the situation. The men left in twos and threes, heading in different directions. The two men I wanted to hear from most, Lester and Dempsey, they said nothing. I wanted to shout at all of them, but nothing came to me. I stood there dumbfounded as they disappeared into the darkness like fireflies, blinking and never coming back. Alma came and laced her fingers into mine.

This woman of mine. She stood five-feet exactly, still wore her hair short, and was just as blunt and practical and energetic as when she was young. After giving birth to three children, helping on the land when she could, she had filled out around the middle, and the hot sun didn't help her complexion any. To me, she was still the warm, beautiful Alma I had married over twenty years ago.

"I really thought they would want to buy the land," I said.

"So they didn't. This is not the end of the world." Her words irritated me. I wondered if she understood how much that valley was a part of me. "We can find other land," she said.

I wanted to shout at her, then what, move every time. Move from place to place just to grow food? That's no way to live. Soon, we'll be growing food out of a pail full of dirt.

"Ezekiel, come see me tomorrow," Grenville said. "This is not over yet. We can still work this out." Grenville shook my hand, gave Alma a peck on the cheek, and went down the road where his car was parked.

I had some trouble sleeping that night. Alma slept with her back to me, her buttocks wedged firmly in my crotch. We always slept that way. I felt the tempo of her breathing. Mabimbay was on my mind. Sleep was far away. The first time we made love was in that valley. Thinking about it then, all those years later, I still felt the same wholeheartedness for the woman.

The next morning I woke early as usual. The thought of leaving the valley congested my mind. I woke James, the younger boy, although I was unsure about whose turn it was to bring back the milk. The boy complained in half sleep and I rough him out of bed. He rose sluggishly and crawled into his clothes.

We had made that trip so many times. This morning it was something else. Could have told the boy that everything would be fine or I'm sorry. Instead, the sound of our footsteps slapped the ground, birds were singing, cocks were still crowing in the distance. The chilly morning air touched my face. Between us, there remained a vigorous silence fasten by my guilt.

Daylight approached as I hunched below the cow pulling on her udders. I handed the pail of milk to the boy. The early morning sun peeked over the trees as he disappeared from my sight. The cattle needed grass. The machete felt weightless slicing through the grass. I swung the sharp steel blade back and forth with speed and rhythm. A green snake slithered out of the grass, body moving sideways, head with darting tongue pointed at me. With one swipe of the blade, I severed the head. The snake curled into a tight knot. I picked up the headless body on the tip of my blade and hurled it over the black sage bush into the cane field.

I returned home before noon that day. Alma fed me a big bowl of Callaloo Melee. I chewed on the

Dumplings and Tannias as I contemplated the future. What could Grenville have in mind? It seemed that everything was over when the men walked away from my plan. Without revealing our mysterious plan to Alma, I changed out of my work clothes, walked down the road, and caught the bus into Saint Georges.

The bus was almost empty on its midmorning trip into town. I sat way at the back, away from the few passengers. The bus sped through Tanteen, then around the Carenage. We pulled into the market place at the base of Tyrel Street without picking up another passenger. I disembarked in a hurry and walked away from the hustle and bustle of the hucksters.

I stood at the base of the steep grade looking up at the road called Market Hill. When I was a boy, I loved running up that hill, the exhaustion and elation I felt after beating all my friends to the top. I felt like running up Market Hill that day, but I thought, no. People might think me crazy if they see me running up that hill in the hot sun with my good clothes on.

I walked up slowly, heading towards Grenville's office. I walked past the old red brick houses mixed in with the newer wooden frame structures painted bright red, pasture green, and jaundice yellow. At the top of the hill, I turned left past the courthouse. Barristers and judges in white wigs and black robes were sitting in judgment on some poor fool who had transgressed the law.

This used to be a favorite walk for me. I especially enjoyed the Catholic Church that sat across from the courthouse. The double-steeple gothic structure with its stained glass windows towered above everything around. I stood in front of the church for a moment. I felt small. The larger than life figures of Jesus and Mary in the bright colored glass had me mildly hypnotized.

The panes contained the form of Mary with baby Jesus cuddle in her arms. On the other pane was the figure of Jesus with a staff in one hand. Lambs surrounded him. I watched as the colors absorb the sunlight. The mild blue blended with the white of the robe and the lambs, the red, green and yellow, all these accentuated the figures. The angle of the sun gave me a strange perspective, one I had never noticed before. It seemed the figures were sneering down at me. I looked around on the ground for an instant. Where's that brick to shatter the glass? The thought vanished as quickly as it came.

I walked on. Grenville's office was in a little house two blocks from the old church. The moment I saw the man, I knew the trip would yield nothing.

"Take a seat Ezekiel," he said. I sat down in a wicker chair across the desk from him.

"I spoke to a man at Beck and Walters in London this morning, Ezekiel. Mabimbay is not for sale. Jacob trying to save face; pretending to sell Mabimbay. The fellow in England said they are anticipating a drop in the price of sugar in the coming years. They want to start a large farming concern, planting vegetables like lettuce, tomatoes, and cucumber, selling them to the hotels on the beach, exporting them to the other islands. They plan to use a method called irrigation, storing water from the river in the rainy season and watering the plants in the dry season. They plan to hire a few of you, to take care of the place, do the packaging. It's a strange business when you don't have control of the land, Ezekiel. We are at the mercy of these people who don't understand that life on this island is all about the land. The way to change this is to vote labor in the next election. I've been hearing some talk about land reform. Enforcing that death tax and reclaiming some of the land, making it available to the people . . . "

The last few words sailed right over my head. Grenville's little speech sounded good, but distant and uncertain. What he was talking about could take years. I wanted results now, action that would settle this, and allow me to return to my life. I stood up and shook Grenville's hand. The man had wasted my time.

The shops, the stores, the faces were all familiar, yet they felt scruffy now. The old school house that I attended as a boy, the place that I hated so much on beautiful sunny days, that old brick building on the bluff overlooking the sea. Suddenly the memory of the place harked back to a young me, protected from the world outside. I decided to skulk around, wait for the boys. We could walk home together.

I started towards the old school with a sincere plan. Looking at my children from the sly was my favorite diversion. It gave me a view of what they were like away from me. I walked by the school, sat under a silk cotton tree a short distance away, and waited for the school day to end. The bell finally rang and the clamor of children erupted. They spilled onto the street like a herd, among the drove were my two boys.

They separated from the crowd the moment they exited the gate. They stood conversing. I couldn't hear them but I watched. James grabbed Henry around the neck. The two boys struggled for a moment then they disengaged, laughing. Henry tapped James on the shoulder and they started to walk, side by side. Their fooling around warmed my heart. I decided to leave them alone, let them enjoy each other for a moment.

My backside felt numb from sitting on the ground under the tree for so long. The wind produced white caps across the sea outside the bay. Glimpses of doubts about the way I had spent this portion of my life creep into me. What if? What if? All the people I had known, those who went to England, the United States or even Trinidad. I envied the risk they took, going out into the world, away from this island. This is all over for me now. Memories are all that I'll have one day. I should have cultivated them better. What can I look back on when I'm walking with a stick? My children. Yes, that's will be my greatest achievement.

The girl, Ruth, she'd been gone over three years, living in England with her husband. I knew she was a grown woman already, but thinking of her that today, I still missed the little girl.

Ruth has always been the pleasant mystery of our life. Being the first of our children, she got all that Alma and I could provide. The little dark eyed girl learned to read early and did great in school. Her considerations were always so much more complex than her playmates.

I was sitting with Ambrose once, talking about a movie we had seen, something about the life of a scientist and his effort to fix the inside of some person's head. This was a picture with lots of talk and no action. Boring, boring. Part of the movie had something to do with memory and we liked that. We sat talking about the various bits and pieces that we forget and remember. The mixtures. The jokes our memories play, especially in dreams. Suddenly a little voice chimed in.

"Its a poor kind of memory that only works backwards."

We looked at Ruth. I had no idea she was listening. "It's like Alice in Wonderland," she said.

And I wished one of the boys were my gifted child.

Another time, at a Shango ceremony, Ruth was probably about fifteen years old. Alma had talked me into spending the money for the ritual.

"Someone worked Obeah on papa," she had said to me. "The only way he could be at peace is if we get it removed."

Deep down, I knew Shango and Obeah was only foolishness, but I surrendered to Alma. We went to the house of the voodoo woman, her aunt.

"Tante," Alma said as soon as we entered the house. "Somebody worked obeah on papa. I'm sure of it. Things are moving around inside of him. I hear them speaking with his voice at night."

The two women glanced at me briefly, and then continued to talk as if I wasn't there.

"I know," the old woman said. "I was wondering when you two would come to see me. You allowed him to suffer too long. Now here's what we need to do . . ."

They conversed in haste. Arrangements for the ceremony happened before I could say a word. One moment we were sitting in the house, the next we were walking home.

"Two days huh?" I asked as we walked down the dirt path toward the house that we shared with my father.

"Yes," Alma answered. "Lots of work to be done."

"I've a feeling that you and your aunt made plans before I came into the picture," I said.

"We spoke about it a little. You know I love Papa," she said.

"You were that sure we would see eye to eye?"

"Yes, I was sure," she said. "You are a man with keen sight."

"Are you trying to treat me like fresh bread, Alma?"

She didn't laugh.

The next day a large tent went up in our yard. The news went out by word of mouth, on the wind through the sound of drums. Alma worked hard gathering, preparing food to feed the many people who would come for three days. She knew the rituals well. All the food must be prepared without salt. The blood of the animals killed must run into the ground. And the Hangan, her aunt, must pick all the herbs used in the flavoring of the foods and in the vigor of the ceremony. The day the ritual began people came early; the drummers, the dancers, and the spectators packed the tent.

The event went on coolly until the evening of the last day. I was sitting with the children watching the dancers and drummers, fingers flailing at the skin of the drum-heads, feet pounded the bare ground into a fine dust. Among the children sat Ruth, watching the ceremony. Alma sat nearby with her aunt.

I stood there in the crowd wondering why I had agreed to all this. Suddenly, Ruth stood and walked into the middle of the dance. The drums stopped abruptly. The dancers formed a circle around her. The drums came back slowly. Ruth stood perfectly still, her body stiff and erect, and then she moved her shoulders. The motion traveled down her back and over her buttocks, then into her legs. Ruth shuffled forward as if her feet were glued to the ground. Her bare feet pushed the fine dirt.

She lifted both her arms into the air and the tempo of the drums build rapidly. The bodies moved together in a swaying undulation of movements, arms, legs, and torso. The dancers began chanting a deep guttural refrain as they moved away in three groups. Ruth danced alone in the middle of the dirt floor, at the mercy of the drums. The rhythm peaked. She moved with it. Her body pulsating, surging to the driving sounds of voices blending with the drums. Her bare feet pounded the ground. Little dust clouds formed, settled back on her feet, turning them a chalky white to the ankles. I stood there, unable to move, confusion racing around in my mind. Ruth danced to an area directly in front of her mother. Ruth and the old woman locked eyes for a long moment, and then Ruth danced away through the crowd into the yard. Alma and her aunt followed. Ruth danced to a stone and dirt path leading into the house. Ruth spit out a wad of saliva onto a flat smooth stone in the middle of the path, and then she slowly crumbled to the ground. The drums went silent. The old voodoo woman reached into a pocket of her dress, took out a vial, sprinkled a red powder into the spittle on the stone, then used her index finger to make a symbol. Then Alma and her aunt lifted Ruth, gently carrying her into the house.

That night, after the ceremony, everyone left. Alma and I lay in bed, in each other's arms.

"I saw you dance like that once," I said into the darkness.

"That was a long time ago," she said.

"I was confused then. I'm confused about Ruth now," I said.

"The spirit came and I had to dance. I don't understand it myself," Alma said.

We were lying there; listening to the night music.

"Ruth started her period today. She is a woman now," Alma said.

I said nothing. I was thankful for the darkness. I didn't want to see her face. But I couldn't shut out the concern I heard in her voice. It left me with a faint uneasiness. Two days after the ceremony my father died quietly in his sleep.

Around four o'clock I left the stop under the tree near the school and started walking towards the wharf where the fishermen came in to sell the day's catch. There were two boats with a crowd around them. "Give me a pound of that Grouper. Give me a pound of that Snapper," the voices belonged to no persons exactly.

"What you doing in town, Ezekiel?" the question came from behind me. I turned and saw the fisherman, Jonas, smiling as if there was a joke somewhere there. "I thought you only come to town once a month." He came toward me and clapped me on the back.

"A man can't spend all his life in the bush. He must come to town now and then, just to see how society is getting along without him."

Jonas laughed. My old school mate, he had left school right after standard six, and started fishing with his uncle Finius. The laughter vanished from his face just as easily as it came. "What's all the grumbling about Mabimbay? What's going on?" he asked.

"The price of sugar is falling, man. The owners want to plant provisions," I said.

"What you talking about?" Jonas asked. His eyebrows arched upwards.

"Let's not talk about that shit anymore. What I need is a good shot of strong rum."

"Let me buy. The catch was good today."

We crossed the street and entered the rum shop. The sound of voices shouting at the fishermen followed us. Bottles of rum and other assorted liquors decked the shelves. The place transmitted a heady aroma, a mixture of rum, cooked and uncooked food, and the stench of rotten bait.

The barman brought us a small bottle of strong rum with two classes and a larger bottle of ice water.

The fishermen sold out quickly that evening. They wandered into the shop in small groups, pockets full of money. The eighths, nips and pints of strong rum kept coming over the counter as the day melted around us. I drank with them until my sorrows were completely forgotten.

The bar finally closed around ten o'clock that night. Jonas and I staggered across the street, and into the fishing boat for the trip across the bay home.

We were halfway home before we spoke a word. The trashing of the oars was driving me crazy. So, I decided to break the monotony with my tongue. Say anything, say anything.

"Jonas, those sons of bitches wouldn't sell. I've the money, but they wouldn't sell. What can a man do? Buy a gun?"

"I'm in doubt, man. Let me think about that." The repeated thrashing of the oars and the squeak of the oarlocks were like music from a stuck gramophone. I sat on the stern waiting on an answer from Jonas.

"You can fish!" Jonas called out after a while. "Yes, you can be a fisherman. They can steal all the land, turn decent men into yard boys, but they can't touch the sea. You can fish with me. It's a good living. And you don't have to pay no rent. I run the long-line, some days..."

The boat hit the shore with a thud. Jonas hauled in the oars and climbed off the bow onto land. I stood up just as Jonas pulled the bow out of the water. The motion threw me back, onto my backside. I pushed myself into a kneeling position and gingerly moved toward the bow.

"Me! A fisherman? I don't even know how to swim, Jonas," I crawled over the bow and stepped ashore.

"That can be a blessing at times," he said.

We hauled the boat out of the water, said goodnight, and Jonas headed his way. I was left alone to stumble home. A little ways down the road I stubbed one foot, staggered and fell forward, almost cracking both my wrists. The ground felt good for a minute as I brushed the dirt from my palms. An owl hooted in the distance.

A million crickets competed with a lonesome drum. Fireflies blinked on and off. The discord came to my ears free of all sentiments.

Jonas was at my side when I stood up.

"Let's go to the house, have something to eat. Might clear your head for the walk," he said.

At Jonas' house, we ate fried Bonita with bread and butter. Jonas brought out a big jug filled with fermented Sorrel. The punch tasted like old red wine. Jonas brought out a bottle of strong rum and poured some into his cup of sorrel. Fifteen minutes after we got to Jonas' little house, we were drunker than before.

I left Jonas' place, intending to go home, but instead I headed toward Mabimbay. I walked, and stumbled, it must have taken me an hour to reach the jupa. I felt sober. A flood of reproach came over me. Those stupid bastards, Ambrose, Atien, Dempsey, all of them, they have no idea, coming here to seek shelter from the storms. No more.

I found the bottle torch, struck a match and lit it. The flame bled off the cloth wick and lit up the space. The dry cane straw, the bamboo ribs. This will burn. This will burn beautifully. I drew back and smashed the torch against the wall of the jupa. The flame jumped up like a dog that had just been roused from a deep sleep. The jupa caught fire quickly. I rushed outside, away from the smoke and the stench of kerosene. The flames engulfed the thing in seconds. A light breeze picked up, blowing the burning embers through the air like fireflies. I walked away, glancing over my shoulder now and then. I wanted to see the fire from the high ridge. I took the path leading to the rocks above the valley.

By the time I made it up to the rocks, I looked down on what appeared to be the entire valley in flames. The wind had blown the fire into the cane. The blaze illuminated the valley. Everything stood out in stark relief, mixed with an orange tinge. Birds took to the sky and flew around, the cows began to low and move around on their pens.

The fire burned quickly. I sat up there and watched it gnaw its way through the cane all down the valley. Around two o'clock it clouded over. Thunder rolled and it rained. It rained a sweet kind of rain that left me renewed. I was ready for whatever.

In the early morning, I left the spot on the hill and started home, determined to get some clothe because the set I'm wearing was wet. I knew in the not too distant this place created by the giant would be gone, transformed into another thing. I knew the law would come seeking explanations about the fire. Things had to be explained, but I have no intention of clearing up anything. I'll never talk to them. I'll hide in these woods and wait, see who come to join me. I'll defend myself from all threat. I'll continue to work land where I can find it, and feed my family. This is what I've become. This is where I'll remain until the Devil come to take me to hell.

ABOUT THE AUTHOR

Claude Alick was born on November eight nineteen forty-nine on the island of Grenada in the West Indies. He's the fifth of twelve children. He was educated in the school systems of Grenada. After graduation, he took to the sea, working as a deck hand on charter yachts for some years before he immigrated to the United States. His experience and education are diverse. He has attended schools in Portland, Maine, Memphis, Tennessee, and Missoula, Montana. His jobs covered a wide range, mechanic, vacuum cleaner salesman and bartender. He lives in Missoula Montana with his wife and child.

Printed in the United States
38082LVS00001B/196-294